RABINDRANATH TAGORE was born in 1861. He was the fourteenth child of Debendranath Tagore, head of the Brahmo Samaj. The family house at Jorasanko was a hive of cultural and intellectual activity and Tagore started writing at an early age. In the 1890s he lived in rural East Bengal, managing family estates. He was involved in the Swadeshi campaign against the British in the early 1900s. In 1912 he travelled to England with *Gitanjali*, a collection of English poems, and won the Nobel Prize for Literature in 1913. Tagore was knighted in 1915, an honour he repudiated in 1919 after the Jallianwala Bagh massacre. In the 1920s and 1930s he lectured extensively in America, Europe, the Far East and Middle East. Proceeds from these and from his Western publications went to Visva-Bharati, his school and university at Shantiniketan. Tagore was a prolific writer; his works include poems, novels, plays, short stories, essays and songs. Late in his life Tagore took up painting, exhibiting in Moscow, Berlin, Paris, London and New York. He died in 1941.

APARNA CHAUDHURI is in her final year at Calcutta Girls' High School.

HE
(*Shey*)

RABINDRANATH TAGORE

Translated from the Bengali by
APARNA CHAUDHURI

Introduction by SANKHA GHOSH

PENGUIN BOOKS

PENGUIN BOOKS
Published by the Penguin Group
Penguin Books India Pvt. Ltd, 11 Community Centre, Panchsheel Park,
New Delhi 110 017, India
Penguin Group (USA) Inc., 375 Hudson Street, New York, New York 10014,
USA
Penguin Group (Canada), 90 Eglinton Avenue East, Suite 700, Toronto,
Ontario, M4P 2Y3, Canada (a division of Pearson Penguin Canada Inc.)
Penguin Books Ltd, 80 Strand, London WC2R 0RL, England
Penguin Ireland, 25 St Stephen's Green, Dublin 2, Ireland (a division of
Penguin Books Ltd)
Penguin Group (Australia), 250 Camberwell Road, Camberwell, Victoria
3124, Australia (a division of Pearson Australia Group Pty Ltd)
Penguin Group (NZ), 67 Apollo Drive, Rosedale, North Shore 0632,
New Zealand (a division of Pearson New Zealand Ltd)
Penguin Group (South Africa) (Pty) Ltd, 24 Sturdee Avenue, Rosebank,
Johannesburg 2196, South Africa

Penguin Books Ltd, Registered Offices: 80 Strand, London WC2R 0RL, England

First published by Penguin Books India 2007

Translation and Translator's Note copyright © Aparna Chaudhuri 2007
Introduction copyright © Sankha Ghosh 2007
Illustrations by Rabindranath Tagore

10 9 8 7 6 5 4 3 2 1

ISBN-13: 978-0-14310-209-0 ISBN-10: 0-14310-209-5

Typeset in Perpetua by Eleven Arts, Delhi

Printed at Repro India Ltd., Navi Mumbai

TRANSLATOR'S NOTE

A child comes to me and commands me to tell her a story. I tell her of a tiger which is disgusted with the black stripes on its body and comes to my frightened servant demanding a piece of soap. The story gives my little audience immense pleasure, the pleasure of a vision, and her mind cries out, 'It is here, for I see!' She knows a tiger in the book of natural history, but she can see the tiger in the story of mine.

—Rabindranath Tagore, *The Religion of Man*

I first read *Shey*[1] when I was ten years old. In retrospect, I think the idea of translating it grew out of a desire to enter more actively into the text and the characters; at the time, it was just something to keep me occupied during a long summer vacation. I approached the translation in no very purposeful spirit—the first draft contained more doodles than writing and was frequently buried under novels, school work and anything else that happened to engage my attention. Done in occasional spurts, the work took longer than it might otherwise have. I changed my mind about almost every sentence, and when, some years later, I completed the translation, I could hardly remember what it was like when I began.

Both while reading *Shey* and translating it I had to keep in mind that the story was originally told and not written (at least, that is the impression sought to be conveyed). Like all told stories, it evolved

---

[1] By the rules of transliteration followed in the book, Tagore's Bengali title should be rendered as *Se*. We have spelt it as *Shey* instead, as being easier on a reader approaching the book for the first time.

through its telling—the ideas are dependent on the words, just as the words are fitted to the ideas. As a reader, I enjoyed this exchange between word and meaning—as a translator, I recognized it as a problem. The hero of Tagore's story is introduced as 'a man constituted entirely of words'. As a translator, I had to create the same man in a different idiom—to tell the same story, but in different words. This search for different words led me to the accidental discovery of many different meanings of the original words; while exploring the linguistic possibility of translation, I was led also to explore different analytic and imaginative possibilities inherent in the original work. Not all these possibilities can be fulfilled, or even conveyed, through translation—they can, however, considerably enrich one's reading of *Shey*. They also make translation of a work like this, more than of any other kind, an imaginative rather than a purely linguistic exercise. If *Shey* is to make sense (or nonsense) in any language other than its original Bengali, merely finding the closest linguistic equivalents in that language is patently not enough to achieve that aim.

At the same time, *Shey* is very much a modern fantasy, part of a universal more-than-real. Like Carroll in *Alice's Adventures in Wonderland* or Antoine de Saint-Exupéry in *The Little Prince*, Tagore taps a vein of the purest whimsy that makes *Shey* a fantasy on the grand scale. Even the local or regional references retain their effect in translation, because they have become components of a fantasy world. At the same time, the colloquial language, the frequent play on words, and the caricatures of the heroes and deities of Indian mythology cannot quite keep their original flavour. I only hope this does not materially lessen their fun.

Happily, the sketches Tagore drew to illustrate *Shey* require no translation, and, therefore, run none of the risks of the text. Yet, at best, they only aid the imagination of the reader, who remains perfectly free to picture Shiburam or Puttulal or the Gandishandung as he or she pleases. In the last chapter, the writer discusses the 'Age of Truth' with young Sukumar and Pupe, when people will know by being, rather than touching or seeing:

Sukumar spoke. 'It's fun to think of you spreading over trees and brooks and becoming part of them. Do you think the Age of Truth will ever come?'

'Till it does, we have paintings and poems. They are wonderful paths down which you can forget yourself and become other things.'

Perhaps the sketches are only the story-maker's way of becoming the story.

This idea of 'becoming the story' is central to *Shey*, a story named after its hero, a man who bears no more distinguished a name than the Bengali third person pronoun (which I have translated as 'He'). We are told that He helps the writer to make up the story: 'I employed another man to help me, and you will know more about him later.' Yet He is undeniably part of the story himself. The story-creator becomes the story's most integral element—a truth behind all stories, but seldom so apparent as in *Shey*. So that the story should include all possible elements, the story-creator does not possess the distinction of a name. His identity and character remain undefined, for to define them would be to limit them—to include him in the unmysterious intimacy of 'you-and-me' when his function is to represent the unknown and exciting 'them'. The ordinary thus becomes the extraordinary, and the ordinary man a creature of untrammelled, whimsical fantasy.

It is this differently fantastic quality that makes translating *Shey* difficult. The language, in itself, is simple, the style easy and conversational, the incidents amusing, even if the ideas, sometimes quite visionary, may seem strange material for a story intended for a nine-year-old. The later episodes give narrative expression to Tagore's thoughts on education, ethics, philosophy and similar subjects that one would not have thought conducive to storytelling. But we must remember that 'in this story of mine, there is no trace of what people usually call a story'. Instead, the very process of story-making is visible and active and, indeed, what the story is really about.

Over five years, as the translation progressed, I grew closer to the story. In fact, I grew with it—or, at any rate, with the person it was originally intended for, Tagore's granddaughter, Nandini (Pupe), the adopted daughter of his son Rathindranath. The first stories about He are, therefore, closer to young Pupe's experience of people and their familiar activities. The 'Shey' of the first stories is, in the writer's own words, 'a very ordinary man. He eats, sleeps, goes to the office and is fond of the cinema. His story lies in what everyone does every day.' No sooner does he enter the story than he makes the endearing confession that he is very hungry, and, as Tagore himself points out, it is easy to make friends with a hungry man. All elements of conventional fantasy are strongly suppressed—there is nothing wonderful or magical about this man, and yet he is to help create a story 'about something quite extraordinary...without head or tail, rhyme or reason, sum or substance, just as we please'. Obviously, the idea is to rearrange the elements of ordinary reality into an extraordinary expression of the more-than-real. It is this more-than-real that we actually experience— Pupe asking for a story 'sees' the tiger in it because the tiger is part of the more-than-real.

Language is not a very important part of this more-than-real, which, paradoxically, makes it difficult to translate. Words are essential to it, but not in their strictly functional capacity of conveying meaning. They become important in themselves—because of how they sound, an inner rhythm or associated image. It is impossible to find a word in a different language identical to the first in meaning, effect and association. At least one of the three factors had to be sacrificed, to avoid every second word being in italics. I faced the greatest difficulty in the twelfth chapter, in which entire poems grow out of just such single, central words.

The part of *Shey* I most enjoyed reading was the poetry. It was also the part I most enjoyed translating. There are two chief sets of poems (not counting stray verses embedded in the text): the 'tiger poems' and the 'tuneless poems'. Each set consists of several poems, on the same theme but varying entertainingly in character and content. The story of the soap-seeking tiger that Tagore alludes to in *The Religion of Man* appears as the first of the 'tiger poems', while the three 'tuneless poems' form a sequence representing a gradual escape from the bondage of metre and scansion to a freer sphere of unstructured expression.

I have always pictured Tagore telling Pupe *Shey* in instalments, as a sort of serial story. Its sudden changes in tone reflect the changes in Tagore's moods and Pupe's demands. As the story progresses, Pupe grows older. When she enters adolescence, the story ends, in a mellow, almost sentimental vein. Sukumar, Pupe's childhood rival and adolescent love, seems to benefit by entering the story towards its close. Pupe fares badly in comparison—in the later chapters at least, she is shown as rather unimaginative, as well as jealous of Sukumar, a representation against which she herself protests.

Interestingly, He disappears from the story in the twelfth chapter: the last two are about Pupe and Sukumar alone. These final chapters were simpler to translate. The story falls into a more natural, human course as Pupe begins to find her own world, the world of people and relationships, both perplexing and fascinating.

It is difficult to discuss *Shey* without doing it a certain injustice. Most critics who wrote about *Shey* when it was first published annoyed Tagore by labelling it a children's book. That he had meant it no less for adults is evident in his reply to a letter from the writer Balaichand Mukhopadhyay (Banaphul): 'Your praise of *Shey* struck me as novel. The book has been consigned to the ranks of children's literature by readers who have looked at it with patronizing eyes. They do not realize how the story has grown like its author—from *aush* to *aman*, from *aman* to *chaitali*.'[2] The translation will, I hope, allow an even larger audience to share in the fun.

*

A few acknowledgements must be made. My parents introduced me to *Shey* and made sure, by their constant support, that the translation

---

[2]*Aush* is the monsoon crop of rice, *aman* the winter crop, and *chaitali* the spring, the richest crop at the end of the harvesting year.

progressed beyond the first page and a half, while my brother Pico's brilliant use of reverse psychology helped ensure its completion. My friends Shriya and Pramita provided encouragement, as always. I sincerely thank Shri Sankha Ghosh, who kindly consented to write the Introduction.

Though there is no formal dedication, this translation is for my grandmother Sujata Chaudhuri. She was more excited than anyone else when I began it, and would have been delighted to see it published.

INTRODUCTION

On one of his journeys abroad, Rabindranath Tagore wrote, in a letter to his nine-year-old granddaughter (3 May 1930): 'Nowadays, I have a great many visitors. Everyone has come to know that I am here. I'd be happy to escape. Why didn't you hide me away in your doll's house?' Childish words, addressed to a child. But is it just childishness? Or is there something else in these words to set us thinking?

In the lives of famous writers, there may sometimes come moments when they wish to hide themselves away—when, suddenly, they feel too exposed to the gaze of the world, too close to its restless strife. Out of this turmoil comes a natural desire to escape to some carefree realm. At these moments the writer may seek refuge in a child-world, approaching as close as possible the sanctuary of that very doll's house.

Rabindranath had earlier expressed the same desire to his niece Indira Debi Choudhurani in a letter dated 10 May 1922. Speaking of his book of children's poems, *Shishu Bholanath* (The Child Bholanath), he confessed, 'There is a great weariness in my mind; I can't easily will myself to take on new cares. A few days ago, I wrote a number of poems for children. The only urge behind them was to remove—if only for a moment—the consciousness of my responsible adulthood from my mind. This sick sense of duty makes a person hard and stiff with maturity. He then begins to despise play, and having eternally sundered play and work, feels pride in having done his duty.' But such freedom deserves to be regarded with something better than contempt; Rabindranath seeks freedom in absorbing that play into his work.

In the relentless creative exercise that occupied his whole life, Rabindranath provided himself with spaces in which to indulge in different forms of play. The book he titled *Shey* is one such creative, carefree space. The dedicatory poem at the beginning of the book says:

Lost to society, the truant scapegrace
Finds his freedom in an unknown place.

The desire to escape from obligation—the obligation to be responsible, the obligation to think, even the obligations imposed by fame—makes this a very different kind of creative interlude.

On the pretext of spinning incredible tales for the nine-year-old granddaughter mentioned earlier, Rabindranath creates a rich and diverse fantasy, openly declaring his desire to 'throw...into disarray' the world of reason and logic. Another creative genius of the Tagore clan, Abanindranath, while making up impossible stories, used the term 'hysteria of the imagination' to describe the process. Rabindranath too, weaving fantasies with his granddaughter, seems to allow his imagination to drift towards the same state of hysteria. Here, a man's pigtail can vigorously grow longer and longer like an endless worm; another wears a broken bucket on his head in lieu of a hat; one might, if hungry, lick the Ochterlony Monument up to its very top; a shovel is employed to clear the eye of coal dust; a brass-bound cudgel is a serviceable toothbrush; and if one's mouth is polluted, the rites of purification are easily looked up in Webster's Dictionary. Creating a commotion with every word, 'kintinabu meriunathu', 'kangchuto-sangchani' and 'iktikutir bhiktimai' announce their presence. The animals found here are strange compounds of humans and cows and lions, which the people of Tasmania have named 'Gandishandung'. Here, if you pull too hard on someone's hair-tuft, his body might well 'slither off him like a loose sock and fall to the ground with a thump', and it is entirely permissible to yell for someone to come and inhabit that cast-off frame.

The little girl who listens to these tales sometimes claps her hands in delight. And sometimes she asks, wide-eyed, 'Is all this true, Dadamashai?'

*

A fantasy in fourteen chapters, *Shey* was published as a whole in 1937, but its component parts had been composed over a long time. Says the storyteller as he begins his story, 'The person who listens to these stories is nine years old.' The young listener—Pupe, or Nandini—was actually ten when some of the parts were first published. By the time they were all brought together as a book, she was sixteen. In one way, though, these story-conversations between grandfather and granddaughter had begun long before Pupe reached the age of nine. She was much younger when, in his diary of that time, Rabindranath wrote (15 February 1925):

> Last night, I had finished dinner and was sitting in my cabin. I was commanded: 'Dadamashai, tell me a story about tigers.' . . . So I began—
>
>> A tiger of the stripy kind
>> A mirror chanced to view,
>> And seeing the black upon his coat
>> Into a temper flew.
>> He thought the matter urgent—
>> So to find a good detergent,
>> Bade Jhagru post to Prague
>> Or else Hazaribagh.

Gradually growing and changing, this rhyme about a tiger would finally come to feature in *Shey*. By then, the artist's strokes and the poet's words had merged to give it a completely different character.

Another being would come to stand between grandfather and granddaughter—his identity left open under the pronoun 'he', unconfined by any definite shape or form, free to wander anywhere and everywhere whenever the fancy takes him. Constantly being born anew, he can say whatever he likes, crossing the bounds between truth and fiction. He can do anything—even write tiger-poems.

In fact, 'He' wanders beyond the confines of the written tale. In letters to the real Pupe at various points in the year 1931, the real grandfather frequently reports, 'He came...He said, "Send me to Darjeeling"' or 'He has gone to Java' or, indeed, 'He went off, saying "Pupu-didi is away, I won't stay here either"' or 'He has gone off wearing my quilted wrap. His own tattered shawl had got soaked in the rain and he's left it behind. I'm thinking of putting it to use as a fruit-juice strainer'.

The telling of tiger-tales to a young listener is a subject Rabindranath returns to in his lecture series *The Religion of Man* (1931), and in discussions of literary theory written in 1933. There he proves how real even the most fantastic tales can be to the child-mind, observing, 'Whatever impresses itself upon the mind in a distinct form or shape is real.' It does not rely upon reason or logic; it may have no functional meaning or factual basis; it may lie far beyond the limits of possibility. Still, 'it presents an image before the mind, awakens an interest in it, fills up an emptiness: it is real.'

Here the word 'real' obviously carries a special significance. To understand what that is, we must consider the literary context of the time. The post-Tagore era of literary activity is about to begin; the young writers of the new age have begun to criticize Rabindranath for ignoring contemporary reality. His works, they allege, are romantic from beginning to end, showing little awareness of the real or existent. Instead, he continues to create a world of illusion, consistently avoiding the harshness of daily life in the real world. At different points in the course of theoretical debate Rabindranath tries to counter such attacks, presenting his own justification. Such debate does not remain confined to theory, but often spills over into his fiction and poetry. Sometimes driven to distraction by the tangles of theory, Rabindranath confesses, 'When these policemen guarding realist literature chase after me, I seek refuge in my songs...and in my painting.' In a letter to Amiya Chakrabarti (24 February 1939) we find, together with those thoughts, expressions of concern at the setting of a market-price on literature, his dislike of 'literary inspectors', and his seeking a sanctuary away from this hostile environment. Again he declares, 'In this precarious situation I still have two stable retreats—my songs and my painting.'

To the two sanctuaries provided by music and art we may add a third—the world of children. Having just experienced the materialism of America, Rabindranath felt compelled to write the poems in *Shishu Bholanath* 'to calm the mind, to make it pure and free'. Similarly, to escape from the agitation and distaste described above, he had to write, one after the other, the verses in *Khapchhara* (Oddities, 1937), *Chharar Chhabi* (Rhyme-Pictures, 1937) and *Chhara* (Rhymes, 1941), and, along with them, the stories in *Galpa-Shalpa* (Stories and So On, 1941) and *Shey* (He, 1937). These works undoubtedly express a wish to escape, an effort to create a world of the imagination fit for young boys and girls. Yet, even here, the same inner trouble, the same conflict with modernity occasionally comes to the surface.

While writing the tiger-poems or the tuneless poems in *Shey*, in moving from one rhythmic form to another, Rabindranath makes it quite clear that he is exchanging thrusts with his modernist detractors. The 'He' of the story tells Pupe's Dadamashai, 'Your honeyed words have trapped you in a stupor, Dada—the harsh truth doesn't please your palate', and informs him, 'The modern age is growing hard and dry.' When Dadamashai asks, 'Why didn't Creation stop once it reached that smooth rhythm?', He replies by recounting the triumph of the hideous over the beautiful, the discordant over the melodious. 'Today Ganesh's trunk has taken the shape of a chimney and is trumpeting over the temples of manufacture in the West,' says He. 'Isn't it the loud tunelessness of that song that's bringing his devotees success?' Hence his prayer: 'Toss my brains with your trunk; let an earthquake engulf my mother tongue; let a turbid force erupt from my pen; let the sons of Bengal wake to its harsh discordance!'

The violence does not end there—we continue to find commands to break out of 'that gentlemanly cut of poetry', 'to beat out the backbones of verses with clubs'. We may even be reminded of the novel *Shesher Kabita* (1929), and the appeal of the poems by Nibaran Chakrabarti, otherwise the novel's hero Amit Ray. Having thrown the ordered world into disarray, stripped the meaning from words and reduced them to senseless explosions of sound, he wants to create a new poetic model. But when, at the end of *Shey*, we hear Dadamashai remark that the discordant and the evil 'pretend to be powerful only to the extent that man is cowardly', or when he tells Pupe, 'Wait another ten years before you venture to judge whether he writes better than I do', we know we are hearing Rabindranath's distinctive voice. It is then that we clearly perceive the nature of the battle between modern tastes and his own. Only then do we understand his pleasure when Banaphul, one of the young writers of the day, observed that *Shey* was more than a children's book.

*

This emergence from the confines of certified 'children's literature' is instanced at several other points of the story. Not only does Rabindranath face up to his modernist critics, but there is evidence that he comes to a conscious understanding with himself. No doubt he wished his words to reflect his whims, to lose himself in 'play without meaning', as he writes in the dedicatory poem. He meant to step away 'directionless/In baul's dress', to bloom as 'a worthless flower among weeds', to fill his work with laughter unrestrained by reason. But is he entirely successful in all this? The question is not the reader's alone. It comes, indeed, from the self-conscious writer. When the story-character He draws the narrator aside and asks, 'Aren't you in need of a little improvement yourself? ... Stop being so old. Here you are, ageing, but you're yet to mature in childishness,' we are witness to an act of self-judgement on the author's part. It is clear that the pieces of advice proffered by He of the story, 'If you imagine you can make Pupu-didi laugh with these stories, you'd better think again!' or 'Leave off your scientific humour and try to be a little more childish if you can', are really Rabindranath's counsels to himself.

Equally evident is the writer's uncertainty as to how this perfect pitch of childishness is to be reached. He recognizes that the story he has created is, in certain places, written 'purely in jest, out of the cockiness of [his] advanced years'. The stories Pupu-didi wants to hear, however, 'are funny without poking fun at anything'. But the presence of satire is not the only problem; Dadamashai distinguishes between two kinds of smiles, one dental and the other cerebral, and says, 'It's the cerebral kind that fell to me—what one calls wit in English.'

Simultaneously, it is driven home to him that 'if you can't stop being so clever, you'd better give up telling stories.' His self-admonition, 'The pungency of your intelligence has dried up all the fun in you', precedes his quest for 'pure laughter without any alloy of intelligence', in other words, the journey towards a new story. Yet even after this, the disbelief in 'Well, then, nitwit, could you make her laugh?', or 'The laughter you win by a cheap joke like that is of no worth', or 'I don't claim that even this story belongs to the highest order of humour', betrays the same self-deprecating hesitation.

The story begins to move away from fantasy towards social satire when, in the tale about the tiger, even Pupe declares she knows how choosy the caste-conscious tiger can be about what he will eat or touch. If a tiger pollutes himself by drinking unholy 'vegetarian blood', the puritanical tiger community demands he perform a penance. And if he refuses? The hapless father of no less than five girl-tigers will be ruined. His five keen-clawed daughters are all old enough to be given away in marriage, but even if he offers twenty-eight buffaloes as dowry, the ritually unclean tiger will fail to procure a suitor for even one of them. A greater punishment awaits him when he dies—no priest will consent to perform the funeral rites, and seven generations of his descendants will bow their heads in shame. What penance, then, can absolve him? He must remain in the south-west corner of the square where the shrine of the tiger-goddess stands, from the beginning of the dark lunar fortnight to the middle of its last moonless night, feeding only on a shoulder of jackal and using only his right hind-paw to tear off the flesh. Reading all this may remind us of Rabindranath's play *Achalayatan* (1912) and its ridicule of absurd rites and conventions. The desire to play truant from society is possibly thwarted by such recurring allusions to the all-too-real world of men.

*

The gradual progress from the world of children to the grown-up world manifests itself in another way as well. As the nine-year-old

Pupe grows into a sixteen-year-old, subtle changes occur in the nature of the story, slowly transforming it. The Pupe who was once ready to believe any impossible thing—who, on hearing of a pen that could make any sum come out right, could clap her hands and cry, 'What fun that would be!', who invented stories about regaling tigers with the dregs of tea in her father's cup, and fretted over the possibility that an Englishman's ghost might starve—is not the Pupe of the story's close. In the tenth chapter, her grandfather tells her, 'Your wits are ripening rather precociously, so today I think I'll remind you that at one time you too were young.' The new Pupe can challenge, 'Let the story be built on a tougher skeleton this time. If we can't slurp it down, we'll at least be able to chew on it. Perhaps I'll like it better then.' A little further on, she comments, 'The young always show signs of age.' Thus, Pupe grows up. The nameless He, who once stood before her fancy, grows older with her. She knows now that He is 'made up', and remarks on his growing up as 'progressing on a line parallel to my own'.

That is not all: another change is now seen in the story. He slowly begins to disappear from it, and his place is taken by a fourth character, Sukumar. The story moves from anonymity towards names; the imagination abandons 'hysteria' for a spellbound, dreamlike state. At the very beginning, the narrator asks, 'Now who is this story about? Our He isn't a prince, but a very ordinary man. He eats, sleeps, goes to the office and is fond of the cinema.' Yet, towards the end he is forced to admit, 'I think we'll have to seek the help of a prince', and that prince turns out to be Sukumar. Sukumar does not himself talk of fantastic things; instead, he wants to hear what the parrot of fairy tales tells his mate. Like the parrot, Sukumar yearns to be where to exist is only to fly, without even a destination to fly towards. Like the parrot's mate, he thinks of the forest full of fruits, flowers and trailing vines, where 'at night, fireflies cast a shimmering veil over that clump of kamranga bushes; and in the monsoon, when the rain comes down in steady torrents, the coconut palms sway and their fronds brush against each other'. Sukumar would like to try being a sal tree and can imagine the murmur of new leaves quivering through his body and drifting up into the clouds. All he wants is to live as one with nature: that is why Dadamashai, facing his audience of Pupe and Sukumar, can keep saying that the scientific mind can accept the coexistence of two opposites; it does not have to choose between 'either this or that'. He can talk to them of the beginning of the world, of life's first foray upon the earth.

Sukumar even hears the story of Dadamashai's encounter with death. 'You know how I used to love Dhiru,' begins Dadamashai, and goes on to describe how he watched Dhiru's death draw close, and how he came to terms with that grief:

> There seemed to be a droning in the sky. I don't quite know why I kept saying to myself, 'From the western sky comes peace, made manifest in night—cool, dark, still. Darkness comes at the end of each day, but today it seems to have a special form and touch.' I closed my eyes, and let the slowly approaching darkness wash over my mind and body, saying inside me, 'O peace, O night, you are my Didi, my sister of ages without end. As you stand waiting at sunset's door, draw my little brother Dhiru to your breast; relieve him of his suffering.'

Dadamashai knows his words will touch Sukumar's understanding, for he is all feeling and imagination, with the creative mind of the true artist. To study painting under Nandalal-babu is Sukumar's dearest wish. When his father refuses to allow it, he secretly escapes abroad, like the madcap Abhik of Rabindranath's story *Rabibar* (Sunday, 1939). Abhik went as a ship's stoker; Sukumar goes 'to train as a pilot'. But both leave behind a few of their paintings. 'For ten whole years, I've practised painting,' Sukumar writes in his diary. 'I've never shown anyone my pictures.' Moreover, he asks Pupe's Dadamashai to show her the paintings and see if he can make her take back her first scornful laugh at his artistic ambitions. If he fails, the pictures should be torn up. As for Abhik, he writes to his left-behind sweetheart, Bibha, 'Nowhere in Bengal will these pictures be valued at a higher price than torn-up paper', but continues, 'just as the thrust of a shovel sometimes reveals hidden treasure, I dare to boast that one day my pictures' priceless radiance will suddenly come to light. Till then, laugh as you will—'

The painter Rabindranath discloses himself through Sukumar's—or Abhik's—preoccupation with art. The last decade of his life, in which he created these characters, was the time when Rabindranath himself turned to painting. It was also the time when he most doubted his claim upon this new creative form that he discovered only in his late years. 'Many ignorant fools have wrongly praised my pictures. And the untruthful have resorted to artifice'—in these words of Abhik's, Rabindranath's own voice is clearly heard. But he did not give himself totally over to self-doubt: a profound inner self-belief was in evidence as well. In one of his affectionate letters to Nirmalkumari Mahalanobis (29 November 1928), he writes: 'Earlier, my mind had laid its listening ear against the sky, it heard the melodies of the breeze, its words; these days it has opened its eyes and exists in the realm of shapes, amidst a crowd of strokes and lines. I look at plants and trees, and see them more intensely—it is clear to me that the world is a great procession of forms.'

It must be remembered that the grotesque is part of this realm of forms. 'Whatever we see,' says Rabindranath in the same letter, 'a bit of stone, a donkey, a thorn-bush, an old woman—anything', if we can, with certainty, see it, 'we touch the infinite'. Just as he paints stroke after stroke in an effort to capture this world of shapes, he also attaches images to his words. This connection between words and pictures is evident not only in the fact that books like *Shey* are illustrated with just such strokes of the author's brush, it exists also in his obvious preoccupation with forms and shapes throughout the story. Hence Dadamashai can tell Pupe, 'I had wanted to be a bit of the landscape, stretched over a wide expanse.' To imagine oneself as an entire landscape seems outlandish to Pupe, but Sukumar's mind stirs in response. He says, 'It's fun to think of you spreading over trees and streams and becoming part of them.'

These roads to forgetting oneself and becoming other things open up in pictures and poetry; by following them, we can arrive at an Age of Truth. Thus utterly releasing the imagination from restraint, Dadamashai ends his story, one in which there is room for both life and death. At the same time, it witnesses the birth of a wistful love. At the story's end, when Pupe hears there is no news of Sukumar, her face grows pale; she goes quietly to her room and closes the door. It is then that Rabindranath's creation, journeying through many realms of the weird and grotesque, finally comes to rest in a 'smooth rhythm'.

*

A young girl has grown up translating this story. Almost at the age when Pupe began her story-conversations with her grandfather, another girl felt encouraged to begin translating them. At first, perhaps, the work was just another kind of play. But slowly, a close intimacy with the text came to be born of playing with it—the translator began to wander off in new directions, in the excitement of discovering new images and word-forms. With astonishing skill, she finished her work at exactly the age Pupe is when the story ends. There must have been a natural sense of identification with the little girl who first listened to the tale, a feeling of growing up with her, beside her.

The work of a translator often takes the form of an intimate and unending exchange between author and translator. Talking to Dadamashai, listening to him, becoming Pupe in her imagination, the young translator's engagement with both the writer and the narrator grows into a rich and fulfilling conversation. It is our hope that this exchange will succeed in conveying Rabindranath anew to an extensive community of readers.

Sankha Ghosh

1

GOD, IN HIS WISDOM, HAS CREATED MILLIONS AND BILLIONS OF PEOPLE, but the expectations of those people are far from satisfied. They say, 'Now we want to create people of our own.' So as the gods played with their living dolls, people began to play with their own dolls, dolls they had themselves created. Then children clamoured, 'Tell us a story,' meaning, 'make people out of words'. So new creations evolved—fairy-tale princes, ministers and their sons, spoilt queens and neglected queens, mermaids, the Arabian Nights, Robinson Crusoe, and many, many more. So many, in fact, that they almost outnumbered the people on earth. Even old men, on office holidays, said, 'Make some people', and the *Mahabharata* was composed, in eighteen volumes. And so, in every country, groups of storytellers set to work.

Recently, at my granddaughter's command, I too have joined these storytellers, and am working on the making of these make-believe characters. They are only to play with, not answerable to truth or falsehood. The person who listens to these stories is nine years old, and the person who tells them will never see seventy again. I began the work alone, but so light and pleasing was the stuff of which these stories were made that, quite as a matter of course, Pupu started to help me in their making. I employed another man to help me as well, and you will soon get to know him better.

Many stories start, 'Once there lived a king.' But I began, 'There lives a man.' Also, in this story of mine, there is no trace

of what people usually call a story. This man didn't cross the field of Tepantar[1] on a magic horse. One night, after ten o'clock, he came to my room. I was reading a book. He said, 'Dada, I'm hungry.'

I've heard many stories of princes, but none of them was ever hungry. However, hearing that this person felt hungry right at the start, I was pleased. It's easier to make friends with hungry people. One doesn't have to go beyond the bend in the lane to make them happy.

I found that the man isn't one to turn up his nose at food. He polishes off a fish-head curry, a dish of prawns with marrows and a plate of vegetables cooked with fish bones. If given sweets from Barabazar, he scrapes the bowl clean. Sometimes he shows a fondness for ice cream. You should see him gobble one—it reminds me of the Majumdars' son-in-law.

One day, it was pouring with rain. I was painting a picture— a picture of the field nearby. To the north snakes a red road, to the south stretches an expanse of wasteland, bumpy and undulating, rather like waves on a beach. Here and there sprout bushy date palms. Far away, a few coconut trees peer imploringly at the sky like beggars. A lowering mass of blue-black clouds had gathered behind those trees, like a crouching blue tiger poised to spring—about to leap across half the sky at the sun and swipe at it with enormous paws. I mixed some colours on my palette and went on painting the scene.

There was a push at the door. Opening it, I saw—not a robber, not an ogre, not even a general's son—but that very man. He was dripping from head to toe with water, and his

---

[1] *Tepantar*: a vast, faraway, mythical plain, often mentioned in Bengali folk tales.

dirty wet clothes clung tightly to his frame. His dhoti-hem and shoes were plastered with mud. 'Now then!' I exclaimed.

He replied, 'I set out in blazing sunshine; halfway here, it began to rain. If you'll give me your bedspread, I'll get out of these wet clothes and wrap it around me.'

I couldn't refuse. He pulled the Lucknow-print bedspread off the bed, dried his hair, stripped off his sodden clothing and bundled himself up in the bedspread. Thank goodness I hadn't brought out my Kashmiri Jamewar[2] quilt!

He said, 'Dada, I'll sing you a song.'

I had no choice. I put down my paintbrush.

He commenced:

Oh Shrikanta, you handsome young charmer,
One day you'll quake in the shadow of Yama.[3]

I don't know whether my expression made him suspect something. He broke off to ask, 'How do you like it?'

I answered, 'You'll have to spend the rest of your life practising the scales, far from the rest of civilization. Chitragupta[4] must take over after that, if he can stand your song in the first place.'

He suggested, 'Pupe-didi[5] learns singing from a Hindustani ustad, how about my joining her?'

---

[2] *Jamewar*: a kind of intricately embroidered shawl or quilt.

[3] *Yama*: the Hindu god of death.

[4] *Chitragupta*: Yama's scribe, who records people's deeds for judgement after death.

[5] *Pupe-didi*: Didi means 'elder sister', but is used affectionately by grandparents to address their granddaughters. 'Pupe' and 'Pupu' are variant forms of the same pet name.

I retorted, 'If you can get Pupe-didi to agree to your joining her classes, there should be no problem.'

'I'm very scared of Pupe-didi, you know,' he confided.

At this point, Pupe-didi laughed out loud. Like the other mighty men of the world, she is always very pleased to know that somebody can be afraid of her.

The kind thing said reassuringly, 'No fear! I won't scold him!'

'Who isn't afraid of you?' I pointed out. 'You drink two bowls of milk every day—think of your strength! Don't you remember the tiger who took one look at the stick in your hand and fled to hide under Aunt Nutu's bed, his tail between his legs?'

Our young heroine was vastly pleased. She reminded me about the bear who, trying to run away from her, fell into the bathtub.

My hands alone had begun to build up the history of this man, but now Pupe keeps adding to it wherever it takes her fancy. If I say that at three in the afternoon he came to my room to borrow a razor and some empty biscuit tins, Pupe informs me that he has made off with her crochet hooks.

Every story has a beginning and an end, but my 'There lives a man' has no end. His elder sister falls ill; he goes for the doctor. A cat scratches his dog Tommy on the nose. He hops onto the back of a bullock cart and gets into a great argument with the carter. He slips and falls at the washing place in the yard and breaks the cook's earthen pitchers. He goes to watch a Mohun Bagan[6] football match and someone swipes three and a half annas from his pocket, so he misses buying sweets from Bhim Nag's.[7]

---

[6]*Mohun Bagan*: a famous Calcutta football club.

[7]*Bhim Nag*: an old and popular Calcutta sweet shop.

At his friend Kinu Chaudhuri's, he devours fried shrimps and spiced potato curry. Day after day passes in this way. Nowadays Pupe contributes to the saga as well. One afternoon, he visits her room and asks her to find the cookbook in her mother's cupboard, because his friend Sudhakanta wishes to learn how to cook banana flowers. Another day he borrows her scented coconut hair oil: he's afraid he's going bald, you see. One day he went to Din-da's[8] house to listen to some singing. Din-da was fast asleep, slumped against the couch.

This 'there lives a man' of ours, he certainly does have a name. But only the two of us know it, and we can't tell anyone else. Here starts the fun of my story. 'Once there lived a king'—he doesn't have a name; neither does the prince. And as for the princess whose hair hung to the ground, whose smile sparkled like jewels, whose tears were like pearls—no one knows her name either. They are not famous, but every household knows them.

This man of ours, we just call him He. When people ask us his name, all we do is glance at each other and smile cunningly. Pupe says, 'Reckon out his name; it starts with a p.' Some say Priyanath, some decide on Panchanan, some think of Panchkari, some insist it's Pitambar, others suggest Paresh, Peters, Prescott, Peer Bux and Piyar Khan.

Arriving at this point, my pen pauses. Someone asks anxiously, 'The story will go on, won't it?'

Now who is this story about? Our He isn't a prince, but a very ordinary man. He eats, sleeps, goes to the office and is fond

---

[8]*Din-da*: the form of address Pupe used for Dinendranath Tagore, Rabindranath's great-nephew, a noted singer and musician.

of the cinema. His story lies in what everyone does every day. If you can build a clear image of this man in your mind's eye, you'll realize that when he sits on the steps of a sweet shop, gulping down rosogollas, oblivious of the juice seeping through the holes in the packet and dripping on to his dirty dhoti, it's a story in itself. If you ask me, 'And then?', I'll tell you how he then boards a tram, finds he has no money in his pocket and jumps off again. 'And then?' Then follow many such events—from Barabazar to Bahubazar, from Bahubazar to Nimtala.

Someone asked, 'Can't a story be about something quite extraordinary, something out of place at Barabazar, Bahubazar or even Nimtala?'

I replied, 'Why not? If it can, it can, if it can't, it just can't.'

He said, 'Very well then. Let this story of ours be just any old how, without head or tail, rhyme or reason, sum or substance, just as we please.'

All this is sheer impudence—going against the divine laws of creation, bound tightly by rules and regulations, where nothing happens that isn't supposed to happen. All this is quite intolerable in the world of make-belief. Let's take the maker of those tedious laws to a sphere beyond the limits of his authority. If we make fun of him there, we needn't fear punishment. After all, it's not his territory.

He was sitting in a corner. He whispered, 'Dada, you can pass off what you like in my name. I won't sue you.'

I must introduce this person to you properly.

The chief prop of the story I've been telling Pupu-didi bears a pronoun for a name and is constituted entirely of words. So I can do what I like with him, without fear of tripping on any awkward questions. But as ocular witness to this uncreated being, I've had to procure a creature of flesh and blood. In a literary law court, whenever the case seems to be getting out of hand, he is ready to bear witness. A signal from a mere attorney like myself, and he blandly affirms that when he went to Kanchrapara for the Kumbh Mela,[9] and was taking a dip in the sacred Ganga, a crocodile seized the end of his holy hair-tuft. It sank without trace, and the rest of him returned abbreviated to dry land. Another wink, and he goes on shamelessly: the pale-skinned divers of a British man-o'-war stirred up the mud of the river bed for seven months and finally recovered the lost tuft, minus only five or six hairs. The divers were tipped three and a quarter rupees. If Pupu-didi still insists, 'And then?', he'll begin on how he fell at Doctor Nilratan's[10] feet and implored, 'I beg of you, Doctor, use what magic ointment you will to fix my holy hair-tuft back to my scalp: I can't tie the blessed puja flowers to my head without it.' No sooner had the doctor smeared on a little of the Thunder-Tangle ointment a hermit had once given him, than the tuft set itself doggedly to growing, like some endless centipede. If our He dons a turban, the turban keeps swelling like a balloon. At night, the gigantic mound of hair on his pillow resembles a devil's toadstool. He has had to employ a barber on a regular salary. The crown of his head has to be shaved clean once every three hours.

---

[9]*Kanchrapara for the Kumbh Mela*: a town to the north of Calcutta. Facetiously said to be a site of the Kumbh Mela, a fair held as part of a pilgrimage in four holy places (Allahabad, Haridwar, Ujjain and Nashik) in rotation.

[10]*Doctor Nilratan*: Nilratan Sarkar, a famous physician, founder of the present R.G. Kar Medical College in Calcutta.

If the listener's curiosity still isn't satisfied, he puts on the most piteous of expressions and continues: At the medical college, the Surgeon General had already rolled up his sleeves, determined to drill a hole through his skull, plug it with a rubber stopper and seal it up with wax, so that no hair-tuft could ever sprout through it either in this life or the next. But he refused, fearing that the operation might pack him straight off to the next life.

This He of ours is rare in the extreme—a man in a million. He has an unequalled gift for inventing untruths. It's my great good fortune to have found such a person to help me make up my impossible tales. I sometimes present this native of Make-Believe-and-Wonder Land before Pupu-didi—her eyes grow round with pleasure when she sees him. In her delight, she stuffs him with specially ordered jalebis.[11] He loves jalebis with a passion, and the chamcham[12] sold in Sikdarpara Lane. Pupu-didi asks him, 'Where do you live?' He replies, 'In Which Town, down Question-Mark Alley.'

Why do I refuse to reveal his name? Perhaps I'm afraid that if I tell you his name, he'll come to rest within his name alone. In all the world, there can be only one me, and only one you; everyone else belongs to 'them'. In this story of mine, He stands surety for all of 'them'.

It would be wrong not to tell you one thing, which is that those who judge him from this drama built up around him judge wrongly. Those who have actually seen him know that he's tall and well built, his features grave. Just as the night is lit up by

---

[11]*jalebi*: a syrupy fried sweet popular in Bengal and North India.

[12]*chamcham*: another popular Bengali sweet.

the glow of countless stars, hidden laughter lurks behind his pretence of gravity. He is a person of the very highest order; all our joking can't demean him. I enjoy disguising him as a fool, because, actually, he's far cleverer than I am. If we pretend he doesn't understand anything, it doesn't hurt his dignity. Rather, it's convenient, as it helps him match Pupu's temperament.

2

PUPU-DIDI HAS GONE TO DARJEELING. HE REMAINS AT SCRUBHEAD LANE in my care. He's moping. I'm irritated too. 'Send me to Darjeeling,' he whined.

'Why?' I asked.

He explained, 'I'm a grown man, yet I'm sitting at home without work. My relatives say all kinds of nasty things.'

'What work are you thinking of doing?'

'Pupu-didi likes to play at cooking, and I'll chop up the paper she cooks.'

'You won't be able to stand such labour. Let's see you keep quiet for a bit. I'm writing a history of Hoonhau Island.'

'Hoonhau? The name sounds good, Dada. It's more suited to my pen than yours. Could you give me some idea of the subject?'

'No joking! It's a very serious subject. I hope to have my essay accepted as a college text. A group of scientists have settled on this otherwise uninhabited island. They're performing a very difficult experiment.'

'Put it more simply, will you—what exactly are they doing? Testing some new method of farming?'

'Quite the reverse. Their work has no connection with agriculture.'

'How do they arrange for food?'

'No arrangements.'

'Then how do they stay alive?'

'That's the most trivial of considerations. They've launched a campaign of resistance to the digestive organs. They've declared nothing's as convoluted as the stomach. The causes of most maladies, wars and robberies are rooted within it.'

'Dada, even if that is true, it's hard to digest.'

'It's difficult for you. But these men are scientists. They've uprooted their intestines, their stomachs have caved in. Food is forbidden; all they live on is snuff. They inhale nutrients with sniffs of air. Some of these reach their insides, the rest are expelled when they sneeze. So both functions are performed at once: the body is purged, and filled up again.'

'How ingenious! I suppose they've set up a huge grindstone. Do they pound chicken, mutton, lamb and vegetables into a jelly and leave it out to dry in huge basins?'

'Certainly not! The entire idea of the digestive system, of abattoirs and butcheries, will be banished. We will be saved the hassle of filling the stomach and paying the bills. The efforts of these scientists will ultimately lead to absolute peace on earth.'

'In that case, agriculture can't be allowed, as that too involves buying and selling.'

'Let me explain. In the living world, the green of the trees is the source of all life. You know that, don't you?'

'A sinner like me can't say so, but if you intellectuals insist, I'm ready to accept the fact.'

'The scientists on the island have extracted a green essence from the grass and dried it in the sun's ultraviolet rays. They've rammed fistfuls of this up their nostrils, just as if it were snuff. In the morning, they stuff their right nostrils; at noon, their left. In the evening, they pack both nostrils full, and that's the main meal of the day. Their combined sneezes have driven disgusted hordes of birds and animals across the sea to the mainland.'

'That sounds good. I've been jobless a long time, Dada, my digestive organs are running amok. If I could start a trade in this snuff at New Market—'

'There's a bit of a problem there, which I'll explain to you later. But these scientists have yet another theory to expound. Because man stands erect and walks on his two legs, his heart and stomach hang to their deaths. His innards have been subjected to this unnatural torture for tens of thousands of years. He pays for this by losing years of his life. Men and women die of their suspended hearts. Quadrupeds, however, need never bother their heads about such dangers.'

'I understand, but what's to be done?'

'The scientists propose that men must learn of Nature's plan for them from babies. On the highest hill on this island, a professor has inscribed these words on stone: "All men must crawl and re-enter existence as quadrupeds, if they wish to prolong their acquaintance with the earth".'

'Splendid! But isn't there something more to this?'

'There is. They remind us that speech is man's invention, not Nature's gift. Our incessant babbling daily shortens our breath, and our lives in the long run. Apes, with their natural intelligence, were the first to discover this. Monkeys, created right in the second stage of evolution, survive to this day. Alone on that desolate island, the scientists have pledged absolute deference to this ancient wisdom. They sit in complete silence, gazing at the ground. On that entire island, not a sound issues from human lips; all one can hear are gigantic sneezes.'

'Re-enter existence as quadrupeds'

'How do they communicate?'

'They've developed an extraordinary code of signals. Sometimes they pretend to be husking rice; sometimes they wave imaginary fans; occasionally they're seized by wild fits of swaying and shaking, like a betel nut tree in the wind. They even write poetry by scowls and winks. Audiences are often moved and where the air is thick with snuff, it gets rather stuf

'I beg of you, Dada, lend me some money. I mu Hoonhau. What a new lark it'll be—'

'Hold your horses. The new hasn't had the chance to grow old yet. The settlement's splitting with the scientists' sneezes. Barrels of green snuff are lying about everywhere. Not a single nose in the place that's fit for human use.'

'You're making all this up. Even science can't let its jokes go that far. You thought you'd astound Pupu-didi with your made-up history of this island. You'd planned to dispose of your luckless He by sending him sneezing round the island in the guise of a scientist. You'd describe how, by ceremonious head-wagging, I enraptured audiences with renditions of those prodigious lyric poems composed to celebrate the slaying of Ghatotkacha.[13] Maybe you'd even marry me off to some crawling, shoulder-waggling island beauty. As the mantras were recited, she'd waggle her head from left to right, and I'd waggle mine from right to left. You'd double the seven steps taken by the wedded couple to fourteen, like the lines of a sonnet. When the islanders filed into the Senate Hall[14] to sit for their exams in the Shoulder-Waggling language, you'd dump me in the corner. You've never shown me any mercy; you'd be sure to have me fail. But in their Sporting Club's crawling race, you'd award me first prize. I'm warning you, if you imagine you can make Pupu-didi laugh with these stories, you'd better think again!'

'Don't jabber so. To make a particular class of people live longer, the sage Chanakya[15] advised, "The fool shall live so long as he does not say too much." I believe you've learnt some Sanskrit?'

'I've forgotten one and a half times what I learnt. A modern Chanakya wrote for the benefit of the whole world, "All heave a sigh of relief when the wise man shuts up." You'd do well to remember it; it matches the earlier rhythm. Now I'm off. My advice is, leave off your scientific humour and try to be as childish as you can.'

---

[13]*Ghatotkacha*: a character in the *Mahabharata,* the son of Bhima and his ogress-wife Hirimba. Ghatotkacha was slain by Karna on the fourteenth day of the battle of Kurukshetra.

[14]*Senate Hall*: a stately building (now pulled down) on the Calcutta University campus, used to hold examinations among other functions.

[15]*Chanakya*: a famous political theorist of ancient times; adviser to Chandragupta Maurya.

This story didn't appeal to Pupu-didi at all. Wrinkling her brow, she objected, 'Is it possible? How could you ever fill your stomach with snuff?'

'But they started by dismissing the entire idea of the stomach,' I reminded her.

Pupu-didi seemed reassured. 'Oh, did they really?'

But the idea of not talking troubled her to the end. 'Can one survive without talking?'

I said, 'The wisest pandit on the island has sent round notices written on leaves, to warn people of the danger of talking. He proved by census that all those who talked, died.'

But a new question had occurred to Pupu-didi.

'What about dumb people?'

'The dumb didn't die of talking, they died of tummy upsets or colds.'

Pupu-didi thought this reasonable.

'What do you think of all this, Dadamashai?'[16]

I answered, 'Some die talking, and some without talking.'

'How would you like to die?'

'I think I'll go and live on Hoonhau Island for a while. On the Isle of Jambu, they nearly talked me to death, I can't stand it any more.'

---

[16]*Dadamashai*: grandfather.

3

HE HAS SENT ME A REPORT OF THE ACTIVITIES OF THE SOCIETY FOR THE Improvement of Jackal Behaviour. I intend to read it aloud in Pupu-didi's company this evening.

REPORT

I was sitting in a field one evening, enjoying the fresh breeze, when a jackal suddenly approached me. He said, 'Dada, you're busy making men of your own offspring. What have I done to be left out?'

I asked, 'What can I do about that?'

'I might be an animal, but can't I aspire to the joys of life? I'm determined you shall make a man of me.'

I thought it would be a worthy deed to rear this poor creature.

I asked, 'What made you decide this?'

He answered wistfully, 'If only I could grow up to be a man, I'd earn quite a name in jackal society. The other jackals would worship me as a god.'

'Very well,' I agreed.

Returning home, I gave my friends the news. They were delighted. 'This will be good work indeed,' they approved. 'The world will benefit from it.'

A few of us got together to form a committee, and we decided to name it 'The Society for the Improvement of Jackal Behaviour'.

There is an old holy porch in our village, fallen to ruin from long years of disuse. We decided to meet there after nine each

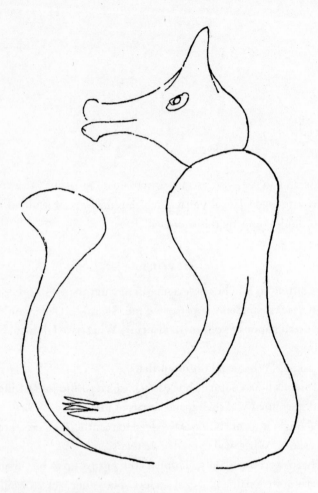

evening, to engage upon the worthy task of making a man of the jackal.

I asked him, 'Young man, what do your brothers call you?'

The jackal answered, 'How-How.'

'Disgraceful,' I said. 'This will never do. We must first change your name, then your appearance. From this day on, your name is Shiburam.'

'All right,' he agreed. But the expression on his face told me that the name Shiburam was not as sweet to his ears as How-How. Well, there was no help for it. He just had to be human.

Our first job was to make him stand on two legs. It took a long time. He tottered about with great difficulty, falling down every so often. It took six months to get him to stay erect. To hide his paws, we made him wear shoes, socks and gloves.

At last our president, Gour Gosai, said to him one day, 'Shiburam, have a look at your two-legged reflection in the mirror. See if you like it.'

Shiburam surveyed himself in the mirror for a good while. He twirled and pirouetted and craned his neck, trying to view himself from every possible angle. Finally, he complained, 'But Gosai-ji, I still don't look like you, do I?'

Gosai-ji pointed out, 'Shibu, just standing straight won't suffice. It isn't easy to be human. What about your tail? Can you bring yourself to sacrifice it?'

Shibu's face went pale. The fame of his tail had spread to a dozen neighbouring jackal-villages. Ordinary jackals called him Fine-Tail. Those who knew jackal-Sanskrit had named him The Furry-Tailed One. He spent two days and three nights in an agony of indecision. Finally, on Thursday, he announced, 'I agree.'

His splendid auburn brush of a tail was cropped close to his rump.

The committee members exclaimed in reverent tones, 'Behold a beast delivered from bestial bondage! At last he is rid of his deluded affection for his tail! He is blessed!'

Shibu heaved a deep sigh and, suppressing his tears, echoed in a small voice, 'Blessed!'

He had no appetite that day. All night, he dreamed restlessly of his lost tail.

The next day, when Shibu appeared at our nightly meeting, Gosai-ji asked, 'Now then Shibu, doesn't your body feel light without that tail?'

Shibu said unhappily, 'Very light indeed. But something tells me that even without my tail, our complexions make us different.'

Gosai-ji answered, 'If you wish to remove that difference between your race and ours, you'll have to sacrifice your fur as well.'

Tinu, the barber, arrived.

It took him five days to coax the fur off Shibu's body with the razor. But Shibu's new-found good looks confounded every one of us.

Shibu asked worriedly, 'Why don't you say anything?'

The committee answered, 'We are speechless at our own brilliance.'

Shibu felt somewhat at peace. He forgot about his cut-off tail and shaved-off fur.

The members closed their eyes and said firmly, 'Shibu, this is the end. Our society is here dissolved.'

Shibu declared, 'Now all that's left is to astonish the jackal community.'

Meanwhile, Shiburam's aunt, Khenkini or Miss Yapper, had been pining for her nephew. She went to Hookkui, the village chief, and said, 'Chief, why haven't I seen my How-How for more than a year? Do you think he's fallen prey to bears and tigers?'

The chief replied, 'Who's afraid of bears and tigers? It's men we have to be afraid of. Perhaps How-How's fallen into their snares.'

A search began. At last, the group of volunteers wandered

into the bamboo thicket surrounding the holy porch. They called, 'Hukka-huaaa…'

Shibu's heart fluttered; he longed to lend his voice to that single-toned incantation. He suppressed his desire with the greatest difficulty.

After three hours, the call came again. A strangled sob rose from Shibu's throat. But he held himself in check.

But when after another three hours the jackals called again, Shiburam couldn't restrain himself. He called back, 'Hukka-huaa, hukka-huaa, hukka-huaa!'

Hookkui exclaimed, 'I hear How-How's voice. Call again!'

The jackals chorused, 'How-How!'

The president of the society leapt out of bed and scolded, 'Shiburam!'

Again the call floated in, 'How-How!'

Gosai-ji warned him again, 'Shiburam!'

But when, at the third call, Shiburam bounded out, the entire search party turned tail and fled. Even Hookkui, Heiio, Hoo-Hoo and the other jackal braves sought refuge in their burrows. The entire jackal community was stupefied.

Six months passed after that.

The latest bulletin says Shiburam has taken to wandering about all night, crying, 'Where's my tail, where's my tail?'

Sitting on the veranda outside Gosai-ji's bedroom, he looks imploringly at the heavens and moans with the passing of each hour, 'Give me back my tail.'

Gosai-ji can't even pluck up the courage to open the door—what if this crazy jackal were to attack him?

Shibu is now forbidden to visit the grove where he used to live, because the other jackals, seeing him approach, either run away or growl and snap at him. He lives in the old holy porch, in the sole company of a pair of owls. Even Khadu, Gobar, Benchi, Dheri and the other young scamps are too scared of ghosts to go looking for karamchas[17] in that part of the forest.

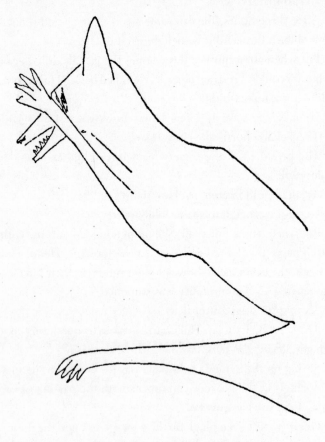

'Where's my tail, where's my tail?'

---

[17]*karamcha*: a kind of fruit.

Shibu has composed, in jackal language, the following mournful ditty:

O tail, my lost tail; without you, I'm now
   Soulless, dead,
      A tailless shred—
How-how, how-how, how-how!

Pupe broke out, 'How awful, what a shame! Dadamashai, won't even his aunt let him back into the burrow?'

'Don't you worry,' I said. 'Just let his fur grow back and she'll be able to recognize him again.'

'But what about his tail?'

'Perhaps we can get some tail-growing ointment from the kaviraj.[18] I'll try to find out.'

Drawing me into a corner, He whispered, 'Dada, don't lose your temper, but I must speak my mind. Aren't you in need of a little improvement yourself?'

'You cheeky rascal, how must I improve myself?'

'Stop being so old. Here you are, ageing, but you've yet to mature in childishness.'

'What's your proof?'

'Look at this report you've just read out. You wrote it purely in jest, out of the cockiness of your advanced years. But don't you notice how sombre Pupu-didi looks? Your story probably sent a chill down her spine. Perhaps she imagined your de-furred jackal coming to complain to her. If you can't stop being so clever, you'd better give up telling stories.'

'It's difficult for me to tone down my cleverness. You wouldn't

---

[18]*kaviraj*: ayurvedic doctor.

understand; you've never had to make such an effort. The Creator is on your side.'

'Dada, now you're getting angry. But I tell you, the pungency of your intelligence has dried up all the fun in you. You think you're being funny, but when your humour gets under the skin, it grates like a scrubbing-stone. I've warned you often enough—in trying to laugh, or to make others laugh, don't risk your comfort in the next life. Didn't you see Pupu-didi's eyes fill with tears at the plight of the tailless jackal? If you like, I'll go and make her laugh right this minute—pure laughter, without any alloy of intelligence.'

'You don't have a written piece ready, do you?'

'I do. It begins in the style of a play. All I need say is that Udho, Gobra and Ponchu of our neighbourhood are talking. Pupu-didi has already made their acquaintance.'

'Very well, let's see what she makes of it.'

THE TREE-SAGE

Udho. Well, did you find him?

Gobra. Brother, after hearing what you said, I've ground my bones to powder this last month, hunting for him in woods and copses, without even a glimpse of his holy hair-tuft.

Ponchu. Who are you looking for?

Gobra. The Tree-Sage.

Ponchu. The Tree-Sage! Who on earth is he?

Udho. Why, haven't you heard of him? Everyone in the world knows his name.

Ponchu. Well, let's hear what it's all about.

Udho. Any tree the Sage seats himself upon is instantly transformed into a wishing-tree. If you stand under it and stretch out your hand, you'll get anything you ask for.

Ponchu. Where did you get the news?

Udho. Bheku Sardar of Dhokar village told me. The Tree-Sage was perched on a fig tree, swinging his legs. Bheku, who was carrying on his head a large pot of treacle to mix with tobacco, passed under the tree in all innocence. The Tree-Sage's dangling leg knocked the pot over, and Bheku found his lips and eyelids sealed with treacle. The Baba is kindness itself; he said, 'Bheku, tell me your heart's desire, and it shall be granted.'

Bheku's a fool. He answered, 'Baba, give me a towel, so that I can wipe this treacle off my face.'

No sooner had he spoken than a towel dropped from the branches. When he was done mopping his face, he recovered his wits and looked up at the tree. But the Tree-Sage was gone. You can only make one wish. After that, even if you rend the heavens with your wails, he won't respond.

Ponchu. Dear, dear, not a shawl, not a stole, just a towel? But then, what sense could you expect Bheku to have?

Udho. That's as it may be. He's getting along quite nicely with just the towel. He's built himself a new house, with a fancy eight-sided roof, at the chariot square. Haven't you seen it?

Ponchu. How can that be? Is it magic?

Udho. The other day, at the Hondalpara fair, Bheku spread out his towel and got ready for business. People flocked to him in thousands. Each time he uttered Baba's name, there was a positive shower of coins, new potatoes and fresh radishes. The women would come to him and beg, 'Brother Bheku, touch my son's head with your blessed towel, he's been ailing with the fever for three whole months.' Bheku's laid down his rule: five quarter-rupees, five whole betel nuts, five measures of rice and five jars of ghee as offerings in return for his services.

Ponchu. They're making their offerings all right, but are they getting any results?

Udho. I should think so! Gajan Pal filled the towel with grain fifteen days in succession; then he knotted a rope to one corner and tied on a goat; its bleating brought people rushing to the spot. In eleven months' time, Gajan had a job. He now prepares the palace guard's siddhi[19] and curls the ends of his moustache.

Ponchu. You don't say! Is this true?

Udho. Of course it's true! Why, Gajan's my uncle's son's brother-in-law!

Ponchu. Brother Udho, have you seen the towel?

Udho. Certainly! Why, you couldn't tell it apart from any other of those Hotuganj weaves, a yard and a half wide, the colour of champa flowers, with a red border.

Ponchu. You don't say so! How could it fall out of the tree?

Udho. That's the beauty of it! By the Tree-Sage's grace!

Ponchu. Come on, brother Udho, come on, let's go look for him! But how are we to recognize him?

Udho. That's the problem. No one's ever seen him. Even that idiot Bheku had his eyelids stuck down with treacle.

Ponchu. What's to do?

Udho. Wherever I go, I say to everyone I see, 'Do tell me if you're the wondrous Tree-Sage!' Hearing this, they charge at me in fury. One fellow even poured the swill from his hookah over my head.

Gobra. Let him. We shan't give up. We've got to find the Tree-Sage—never mind what it takes.

---

[19]*siddhi*: an intoxicating drink made from Indian hemp.

Ponchu. Bheku says the Tree-Sage can only be seen on a tree. Down on the ground, there's no way of knowing him.

Udho. You can't test people by making them climb trees, brother. I had a brainwave. My hog-plum tree was laden with fruit, and I said to everyone I saw, 'Come, climb the tree and help yourself to all the fruit you want.' The tree's been stripped bare, the branches are wrecked, but I've yet to spot this elusive tree-climber.

Ponchu. There's no time to waste—let's get going. With luck, we're bound to get a glimpse of the sage. Why not call upon him, 'Tree-Sage, O Tree-Sage, kind and compassionate Tree-Sage, if you're lurking somewhere in these parul woods, do appear before us unhappy mortals.'

Gobra. That's enough! The Tree-Sage has had mercy upon us!

Ponchu. Where, where?

Gobra. Why, on that chalta tree over there!

Ponchu. What? I don't see anything!

Gobra. Why, can't you see it swinging?

Ponchu. Swinging? But that's a tail!

Udho. Have you lost your wits, Gobra? That's not the Tree-Sage; it's a monkey! Don't you see it pulling faces at us?

Gobra. It's a dark age, you see. The Tree-Sage has disguised himself as a monkey to trick us.

Ponchu. We're not deceived, your black face can't deceive us! Make as many faces as you like, we're not budging from this spot—we have sought the refuge of your holy tail.

Gobra. Look! The sage is leaping away! He's trying to give us the slip!

Ponchu. That's impossible! Can he ever outrun our devotion?

Gobra. There he is, sitting on top of that bael tree!

Udho. Go on, Ponchu, climb the tree!

Ponchu. Why don't you climb it?

Udho. No, you climb it.

Ponchu. We can't ascend to your height, Baba. Have mercy on us and come down.

Udho. Bless us, holy Tree-Sage. In our last hours, may we close our eyes with your holy tail round our necks.

'Well then, nitwit, could you make her laugh?'

'No. It's not easy to make a person laugh who believes unquestioningly in everything. In fact, I'm feeling rather apprehensive: what if Pupu-didi sends me in search of the Tree-Sage?'

The look on Pupu-didi's face caused me a twinge of misgiving as well. The idea of the Tree-Sage obviously appealed to her. Well, tomorrow I'll conduct a little experiment, and find out if it's possible to have a bit of fun over something without believing in it.

After a while, Pupu-didi came to me and asked, 'Dadamashai, what would you have asked the Tree-Sage for?'

I answered, 'I'd ask him for a magic pen that would make all Pupu-didi's sums come out right.'

Pupu-didi clapped her hands and cried, 'What fun that would be!'

This time, in her arithmetic exam, Pupu-didi has scored thirteen and a half out of a hundred.

4

I DON'T KNOW IF I'M AWAKE OR DREAMING. I DON'T KNOW HOW LATE IT is. The room is dark; the lantern stands outside in the veranda. A small bat is wheeling about the room, greedy for insect prey, like an unappeased spirit.

He arrived and yelled out, 'Dada, are you asleep?' Without waiting for an answer, he burst into the room. He was shrouded from head to toe in a black rug.

'What's this you're wearing?' I demanded.

'It's my wedding suit,' he answered.

'Your wedding suit! Explain!'

'I'm going to see my bride.'

I don't know why, but my sleep-befuddled senses found nothing inappropriate in his attire. I exclaimed enthusiastically, 'You're admirably garbed. I'm pleased to note your originality. Your costume is nothing short of classical.'

'What do you mean?'

'When Shiva married his ascetic bride,[20] he was draped in elephant hide. You're in bearskin. Close enough. The sage Narada[21] would have approved.'

---

[20] *When Shiva married his ascetic bride*: Shiva's consort Parvati won her husband through long and severe penance.

[21] *Narada*: an ancient sage of great wisdom and musical prowess, but also known for his bad temper and contentiousness.

'Dada, you're a sensible man. That's why I came to you, even at this hour of the night.'

'How late is it?'

'No later than one-thirty, I think.'

'Must you visit your bride right now?'

'Right now.'

Hearing this, I cried, 'Splendid!'

'Why?'

'I can't imagine why the idea didn't occur to me sooner. You view your office boss in the glare of day, and your wife in the darkness of night.'

'Dada, your words are like nectar. Give us an example from the scriptures.'

'Just think of Mahadeva[22] staring at Mahakali[23] in wonder, in the inky darkness of a moonless night.'

'Oh, Dada, your words make my spine tingle. Sublime, as they say. In that case, we mustn't waste time on words. Let's be off.'

'Who is the bride, and where is she?'

'She's the younger sister of my sister-in-law. She's at my sister-in-law's house.'

'Does she resemble your sister-in-law in appearance?'

'I'd say. It's obvious they're sisters.'

'In that case, there is need of a dark night.'

'My sister-in-law's told me herself, "You mustn't bring your electric torch." '

'Where does your sister-in-law live?'

---

[22] *Mahadeva*: another name for Shiva.

[23] *Mahakali*: goddess of destruction; an incarnation of Durga.

'Twenty-seven miles from here—in the Unkundo quarter of Chouchakla village.'

'Will there be a feast?'

'Certainly.'

I was seized by I don't know what giddy delight. My liver has caused me untold suffering for twelve years—the very mention of food makes me bilious.

I asked him, 'What will the food be like?'

He answered excitedly, 'Delicious, delicious, delicious! My sister-in-law makes a wonderful stew of mango jelly and boiled bitter-gourd, and a chutney of kul seeds ground in a paddy-press, mixed with tobacco-leaf juice—'

So saying, he began to dance in English fashion—*ti-ti-tom-tom, ti-ti-tom-tom, ti-ti-tom-tom!*

I have never danced in my life, but I was suddenly possessed by a wild desire to join him. The two of us linked arms and began prancing—*ti-ti-tom-tom*...

I felt extraordinarily light-footed; if Jamuna-didi had seen me, she would have been impressed.

Finally, out of breath, I sat down heavily. 'That sumptuous menu you recited, why, it's nothing but vitamins. Nectar for the liver. You're going to see your bride, but she must be tested first.'

'There's been a round of testing already.'

'How was that?'

'Well, I thought, before we're eternally matched, let's find out if we match at all. Tell me if that wasn't wise.'

'Wise it was. But what method did you employ?'

'I thought we should see if we could match verses. I sent the

assistant editor of the *Rangmashal*[24] to represent me. He began:
"Beauty, you're as dark as night."

'"Give me a rhyme that matches this," he challenged. "A
perfect match, mind."

'The bride reeled off in a single breath:

You're almost blind, so dim your sight.

'The assistant editor found this intolerable. He retaliated:

Long-armed Brahma[25] in the night
Made you at the cease of light.

'What made him say "long-armed"?'

'I've heard the girl is tall. She must be a good two inches
taller than you. That's the main reason for my ardour.'

'You can't be serious!'

'Marry one wife, and get half an extra one thrown in.'

'I admit I hadn't looked at it that way.'

'Anyway, having submitted to defeat at the hands of the
assistant editor, she has pledged submission.'

'A bond?'

'Yes, she's strung fish-scales on a thread to make a necklace,
and put it round his neck, saying: "The scent of fame will follow
you to the ends of the earth."'

I leapt to my feet, exclaiming, 'I am indeed fortunate! I see
this will be a marriage of one exceptional person to another.

---

[24]Rangmashal: a popular children's magazine of the time.

[25]*Brahma*: one of the principal Hindu gods; the creator of the universe, while
Vishnu is the preserver and Shiva the destroyer.

Such an event is rare in the extreme! In that case, why hunt for an auspicious day and hour?'

'But the girl has laid down a condition. Whoever defeats her receives her hand in marriage.'

'What do you have to beat her in? Looks?'

'No, in matching words. If I can match my words with hers, she's prepared to resign herself to me.'

'Are you sure you'll be able to do that?'

'Of course.'

'Let's hear your plan.'

'I'll say, "Describe my character in four lines. Your ode must please me. The rhyme must be a perfect match." '

'If one could take out patents on methods of bride-choosing, you'd have been a sure candidate. A hymn to the groom, just to begin with! This was how the goddess Uma won in the end!'

'We must prompt her with the first line, otherwise she won't have an inkling of my character. The beginning of the ode is to be: "As a man, I perceive you're extremely queer."'

'If we insist on a perfect match of three entire lines, the girl will hold her head in her hands in despair. She'll just have to admit defeat. Let's hear *you* give us the next line, Dada.'

I recited:

You're possessed by a demon, such is my fear.

'Excellent! But the poem will be incomplete without a few more lines. I'd say, forget the bride, not even her father could find lines to match these. Dada, can you think of anything, sense or nonsense?'

'Nothing at all.'

'Then listen—

Jump off the roof with a thud,
Land on your head in the mud;
Just as the fit takes you, any-how-where.'

'What on earth is that? Where do they speak such a language?'

'Why, it's Sanskrit, the language of the gods—at a stage when it had not progressed beyond strange noises.'

'Any-how-where—what does that mean?'

'It means, whatever you like. Just as you please. That's in Bengali. Modern scholars call it a verbal legacy.'

My reverence for the fellow overflowed its banks. He had extraordinary potential in him. I thumped him on the back and told him he had stunned me.

'It won't do to stay stunned,' he declared. 'We must get going. The auspicious hour set for the wedding is passing. The hour of Babakaran will pass, then Taitilakaran, then Vaishkumbhajog, and after that, Harshanjog, Bishtikaran, and in the end, Asrikjog and Dhanishthanakshatra.[26] The Goswamis[27] maintain that when Vyatipatjog, Balakaran and Parighjog coincide with Garkaran, disaster is imminent. A housewife knows no greater danger than Garkaran. Siddhijog, Brahmajog, Indrajog, Shivajog—none of them occur this week. There's a faint hope of Bariyanjog, if the seventh of the twenty-seven stars appears in the sky.'

---

[26]*Babakaran, Taitilakaran, Vaishkumbhajog, Harshanjog, Bishtikaran, Asrikjog, Dhanishthanakshatra*: words mocking the rigmarole of Sanskritic terms of ritual and ceremony.

[27]*Goswami*: a common surname or appellation of Vaishnavs.

'No more delay. We must set off immediately. Shout for Puttulal, tell him to bring his motorcar. He'll have sat down at his spinning wheel by now. He can't sleep without spinning a while; that's what driving has done to him.'

We climbed into the car.

We were driving through a forest. It was very dark. A jackal howled somewhere among the thick clumps of weeds guarding a pond. It must have been about half past three in the morning. The noise gave Puttulal such a shock that he drove the car straight into a pool of water. Meanwhile, a frog had got into his clothes and was hopping around wildly in the region of his back. What a shrieking he set up! I tried to soothe him by saying, 'Puttulal, you keep complaining of backache. Let the frog jump about all it likes, you'll never get such a fine massage for free!'

I clambered up on to the roof of the car and began calling, 'Banamali, Banamali!'

Not a sound from the stupid fellow. It was clear he was bundled up in a rug on the platform at Bolpur[28] station, snoring loudly. I felt strongly inclined to go tickle his nose with a fountain pen and make him sneeze. Perhaps that would wake him up.

Meanwhile, my hair was drenched in muddy water. I couldn't possibly present myself at our friend's sister-in-law's without combing it properly. Roused by the hullabaloo, the ducks by the pond had set up a furious honking. With a single bound, I landed among them and, grabbing one, scrubbed vigorously at my head with its wing. That restored my hair to some degree of order. Puttulal suddenly remarked, 'You were right, Dadababu. That frog

---

[28]*Bolpur*: a town (originally a village) near Shantiniketan. The railway station for Shantiniketan is situated here.

Puttulal

hopping over my back is really making me feel quite comfortable. I'm beginning to feel rather drowsy.'

We finally reached He's sister-in-law's house. I was so hungry that I'd completely forgotten about meeting the bride. I asked his sister-in-law, 'He was with me all this while, why don't I see him now?'

His sister-in-law's dulcet tones issued through three yards of swaddling dupatta: 'He has gone to seek his bride.'

'In what dump?'

'In the bamboo thicket by the dried-up pond.'

'How far away would that be?'

'A nine-hour journey.'

'Not very far, then. But I'm famished. Bring out that chutney of yours.'

Sister-in-law lamented in nasal tones, 'Curse my ill-luck, it was only the Tuesday before last that I filled the shell of a burst football with all that was left of it and sent it off to Buju-didi. She loves it so with mustard oil, chillies and gram-flour dumplings.'

My face went pale. 'What'll we eat, then?'

Sister-in-law answered, 'Shrivelled shrimps in treacle syrup. Do eat something, son, or you'll have a stomach ache.'

I ate what I could, but there was a lot left. 'Have some?' I asked Puttulal.

He answered, 'Give me the jar, I'll take it home and eat it after evening prayers.'

We came back home. Our sandals were soaked and we were plastered in mud.

I summoned Banamali. 'You monkey, what were you doing when we called you?'

He burst into tears and sobbed, 'A scorpion had stung me, and it sent me straight to sleep.'

Having said this, he trotted back to bed.

Suddenly, a villainous-looking fellow burst into the room. He was very tall, broad-shouldered and barrel-necked; as dark as Banamali, with bushy hair and bristling whiskers. His eyes were bloodshot, and he was dressed in a printed smock, with a three-cornered yellow towel knotted around his striped red lungi.[29] In his hand was a bamboo cudgel topped with long copper spikes. His voice was like the horn on Gadai-babu's motorcar. His bellow of 'Babumashai!' would have turned the scales at no less than three and a half maunds.

I flinched, tearing a hole in my paper with a nervous thrust of my pen.

'What's the matter?' I demanded. 'Who are you?'

He answered, 'My name is Pallaram. I've come from my sister's house. Where's that He of yours?'

I said, 'How should I know?'

Pallaram glowered at me. 'Don't know, indeed!' he shouted. 'I can see that single sock of his—the patched, hairy, green one— dangling from your bookshelf like the chopped-off tail of a dead squirrel. How would he bring himself to leave that behind?'

I said, 'Our He isn't one to sustain losses. Wherever he's gone, he's sure to come back for it. But what's the matter?'

He replied, 'Yesterday, my sister went to the house of the commander-in-chief of the army and made a pact of friendship with his wife. She returned to discover that your He had made off with a pot, an umbrella, a deck of playing cards, a hurricane lantern and a sack of anthracite coal. She can't even find the basket of bamboo sprouts, tender ends of bottle-gourd and cane-bush leaves that she'd brought in from the garden. She's simply furious.'

---

[29]*lungi*: a length of cloth worn wrapped round the waist by men.

'Well, what am I to do about that?' I asked.

'That He must be hiding somewhere on your premises, bring him out!' ordered Pallaram.

'He isn't here,' I protested. 'Go lodge a complaint at the police station.'

'He must be here.'

'This is a pretty kettle of fish! I tell you he isn't here!'

'He must be here, he must, he must!' Pallaram pounded on my table with his brass-topped cudgel. The madman next door began howling like a jackal. All the neighbourhood dogs began yapping. Banamali had left me a glass of bael sharbat, which Pallaram now knocked over. The juice mingled with violet ink from a smashed bottle and ran gracefully down the silk sheet to puddle in my shoes. I began yelling for Banamali.

As soon as he saw Pallaram, Banamali fled, calling upon his ancestors to save him.

I suddenly remembered. 'Our He has gone to find his bride.'

'Where?'

'In the bamboo thicket by the dried-up pond.'

The giant exclaimed, 'Why, that's where I live!'

'That's all right, then. Do you have a daughter?'

'I do.'

'Well, now you've found her a suitor.'

'I can't be quite sure yet. I'll stand over your He with my cudgel till they're married. Only then will I consider myself relieved of my paternal responsibility.'

'Well then, you'd better be off. You mightn't see the groom around, now that he's seen his bride.'

'Right you are,' he agreed.

There was an old broken bucket in the room. He seized it. 'What will you do with that?' I asked.

'It's very sunny outside,' he explained. 'This'll do for a hat.'

He went off. By then, the crows had started cawing, and I could hear the trams rumbling by. I sat up hurriedly and called for Banamali.

'Who was it that entered this room?' I demanded.

'Didimani's cat,' Banamali answered, rubbing his eyes.

At this, Pupu-didi looked bewildered. 'Why, Dadamashai, all this while you've been telling me how you went to a feast and were visited in your room by Pallaram.'

I stopped myself just in time. I had been about to explain wisely that I had dreamt it from start to finish. That would have ruined it all. From now on, I would have to manage Pallaram as best I could. When the Creator interrupts our dreams, it doesn't do to complain. When we do it ourselves, it seems most unkind.

Pupu-didi reminded me, 'Dadamashai, you still haven't told me whether they got married.'

I realized a wedding was necessary. 'There was no way they could escape it!' I told her.

'Did you meet them after their marriage?'

'I certainly did. It was half past four in the morning. The gas lamps on the streets were still burning. I saw the bride marching her husband along.'

'Where to?'

'To New Market, to buy some yams.'[30]

---

[30]New Market was a fashionable European-style market. One would not go there to buy something as rustic as yams.

The bride marched her husband to New Market to buy some yams

'Yams!'

'Yes. Mind you, the groom had objected.'

'Why?'

'He'd said he'd buy a jackfruit if they really needed it, but he wasn't equal to yams.'

'What happened after that?'

'Our unfortunate He had to lug the big yam home on his shoulder.'

Pupu was pleased. She said, 'Serve him right!'

5

I WAS SIPPING MY TEA IN THE MORNING, WHEN HE TURNED UP.

'Got anything to tell me?' I asked.

'I do,' he said.

'Well, tell me quick, because I have to be off in a minute.'

'Where to?'

'The viceroy's.'

'Does he often send for you?'

'No, he doesn't, but he would do well to.'

'Why?'

'He'd have found me a greater expert at inventing news than all his informants. No Rai Bahadur[31] could ever measure up to me, as you know.'

'I know, but nowadays you're saying whatever you like about me.'

'There's a demand for fantastic tales, you see.'

'Fantastic they may be, but even fantasy has its limits. Anybody could put together a string of commonplace, jumbled-up inventions.'

'Let's have a sample of your fantasy.'

'All right, listen—'

Scholarly Smritiratnamashai,[32] the Mohun Bagan goalkeeper, had swallowed five goals in succession from the Calcutta team. But

---

[31] *Rai Bahadur*: a title given by the British Raj to Indians considered loyal to it.

[32] *Smritiratna*: a degree awarded to Sanskrit scholars versed in the Smritishastras.

Smritiratnamashai

far from satisfying his appetite, they made his stomach growl
for more. He found himself in front of the Ochterlony
Monument.[33] He began by licking the bottom, but soon he had
licked it up to its very tip. Badruddin Mian, cobbling shoes in the
Senate Hall of the university, saw him and rushed out in horror.
'You're learned in the sacred books, and yet you contaminate
this great monument with your spittle!' he scolded. 'Fie, fie!'

He then himself spat thrice upon the monument and hurried
off to report the matter at the Statesman House.[34]

Smritiratna suddenly regained his wits. He realized his mouth,
too, had been polluted by the monument.

He went to the guard at the museum gate, and said, 'Pandey-
ji, you're a Brahmin like me, you must do me a favour.'

'*Comment vous portez vous, s'il vous plait?*'[35] answered Pandey-ji,
twirling his goatee and touching his cap in a salaam.

'That's a very difficult question,' said the pandit, after some
thought. 'I'll look up the *Sankhyakarika*[36] and tell you tomorrow.
In any case, my mouth has been polluted today. I licked the
monument.'

Pandey-ji struck a match and lit himself a Burma cheroot. He
took two deep puffs and ordered, 'Go home immediately, and
look up the ritual of purification in Webster's Dictionary.'

---

[33]*Ochterlony Monument*: a tower in the heart of Calcutta, named after Sir David
Ochterlony, a soldier and administrator of the Raj. Now called Shahid Minar
or Martyrs' Tower in memory of India's freedom fighters.

[34]*Statesman House*: the office of the well-known newspaper, *The Statesman*.

[35]Commez vous portez vous...: 'How are you, if you please?' The comic use
of French is found in the original.

[36]Sankhyakarika: the most important text of the Sankhya school of philosophy;
written by Ishwara.

'I'll have to go all the way to Bhatpara[37] for that,' protested Smritiratna. 'It can wait. Meanwhile, I want you to lend me that brass-bound cudgel of yours.'

'What for?' asked Pandey. 'Got a speck of coal dust in your eye?'

'How did you know?' replied Smriratna. 'It happened the day before yesterday. I had to rush off to Ultadingi, to consult the famous doctor MacCartney-saheb; he specializes in complaints of the liver. He sent for a shovel from Narkeldanga and scraped the eye clean.'

Pandey-ji asked, 'But why do you need my cudgel?'

'It'll serve for a toothbrush,' answered the pandit.

'Oh, that's all right, then!' exclaimed Pandeyji in relief. 'I thought you were going to stick it up your nose to bring on a sneeze. In that case, I'd have had to purify it with Ganga water.'

Having reached this point, He pulled the hubble-bubble closer and inhaled deeply. 'You see, Dada, this is your way of telling stories. Instead of tracing them out clearly and simply with your forefinger, you write them out in exaggerated curves and flourishes, as if you had Lord Ganesh's trunk for a pen.[38] You must twist the familiar into the strange. It's very easy. People might laugh when you say the viceroy's set up trade in oil and is selling dried fish at Bagbazar, but the laughter you win by a cheap joke like that is of no worth.'

---

[37]*Bhatpara*: a place to the north of Calcutta, famous for its Brahmin scholars and priests.

[38]Ganesh, the elephant-headed god, inscribed the *Mahabharata* to the poet Vyasa's dictation.

Pandey-ji

'You seem out of temper.'

'With good reason. The other day, you made up a string of stupid stories about me and reeled them off to Pupu-didi. Being a child, she swallowed it all. If you must tell fantastic tales, put some craftsmanship into the telling.'

'You're telling me there was no craftsmanship in my story?'

'None at all. If you hadn't got me involved, I would have kept quiet. But if you insist you'd treated your guest to curried giraffe, whale fried in mustard paste, pulao with a hippopotamus dragged kicking from the mud and stir-fried stumps of palm trees, I can't but call it clumsy. Anyone can write like that.'

'Well, how would you write if you had to?'

'Are you sure you won't be vexed? Dada, it's not as if my powers of invention are any greater than yours. If it had been me, I'd have said—"I was invited to play cards in Tasmania,[39] a simple game of dekha-binti.[40] The man of the house, Kojmachuku, and his missus Shrimati Hanchiendani Korunkuna had a daughter called Pamkuni Devi; she had cooked us a kintinabu meriunathu with her own fair hands. You could smell it seven blocks away. The aroma excited the jackals so much that they threw caution to the winds and began howling in broad daylight— whether from greed or disgust, I couldn't tell. The crows drove their beaks into the ground, got stuck and flailed their wings in despair for a good three hours. That's just the vegetables. There were great barrels of kangchuno-sangchani to follow.

---

[39]*cards in Tasmania*: in the original, the phrase is a pun on 'taash' (the Bengali word for cards) and Tasmania.

[40]*dekha-binti*: a card game where one scores extra points by holding three high-value cards in sequence.

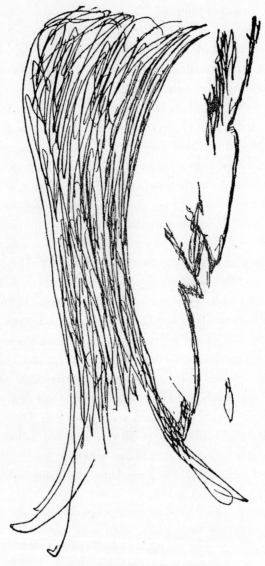

Shrimati Hanchiendani Korunkuna

There was chewed peel of aankshuto, a fruit very popular in that region. And for dessert, there was a basketful of iktikutir bhiktimai.

'"First their pet elephant came and pulped all this under his great feet. Then the largest animal of their land, the gandishangdung, as they call it—a cross between a man, a bull and a lion—came and licked the mixture with his spiky tongue, till it was a soft mush. Then they struck up a fearsome hammering of mortar and pestle before the three hundred expectant guests. The people there insist on this racket as a kind of appetizer; the noise brings in hordes of beggars from the distant reaches of the town. Those whose teeth are wrenched off as they eat donate their broken molars to the host before leaving. He stores them away in the bank and leaves them to his sons in his will. The more teeth one possesses, the greater one's reputation. Many even steal the teeth collected by others and pass them off as their own. People have fought fiercely over this in court. A man who owns a thousand teeth will never give his daughter in marriage to someone with only fifty. If the insignificant possessor of just fifteen teeth suddenly chokes to death on a ketku sweet-ball, you won't find a man in the Neighbourhood of the Thousand-Toothed who'll stoop to cremating the body. The corpse has to be furtively floated off in the Chouchingi River. But now the people who live on its banks have begun to demand compensation; the battle has gone as far as the Privy Council."'

By this time, I was panting for breath. 'Stop, stop,' I gasped. 'But let me ask you what's so special about the story you've just told me.'

'It's special because it isn't just some chutney of pulped kul seeds. No one can complain if you feed your appetite for

Gandishangdung

exaggeration by enlarging upon the impossible. Of course, I don't claim even my story belongs to the highest order of humour. Only a story that makes you believe in the unbelievable can be said to have that extraordinary charm. I warn you, you'll end up in disgrace if you go on with shoddy exaggerations only good enough to hush a crying child.'

'All right, from now on I'll tell Pupu-didi such stories that we'll need an exorcist to drive out her faith in them.'

'Good, but what did you mean by saying you were going to the viceroy's house?'

'I meant I wished to be rid of your presence. Once you sit down, you show no sign of getting up. It was just a polite way of saying, "Scoot!" '

'I see. I'll be getting on, then.'

6

AFTER A TRIP TO THE CIRCUS, PUPU-DIDI'S BRAIN SEEMS INFESTED BY tigers. She often meets tigers, to say nothing of their aunts. Their gatherings liven up only in our absence. The other day she came to ask me if I knew of a good barber.

'What do you want a barber for?' I asked her.

Pupu informed me that a tiger had become a perfect nuisance, pestering her about his whiskers. They had become too bushy; he wanted a shave.

'What put the idea into his head?' I asked.

'Each morning, after Father's drunk his tea, I give the tiger the dregs left in the cup,' Pupu explained. 'That day, when he came for his drink, he caught sight of Panchu-babu. He's convinced he'll look exactly like Panchu-babu once he's had a shave.'

I said, 'He isn't entirely wrong in thinking that. But there's a problem. What if he finishes off the barber before the unfortunate fellow can finish off the shave?'

Pupu-didi had a brainwave. 'You know, Dadamashai, tigers never eat barbers.'

'What!' I exclaimed. 'Why not?'

'To eat a barber is a sin.'

'Excellent, we needn't worry. We'll take him to the English hairdresser on Chowringhee.'[41]

---

[41]*Chowringhee*: an area in central Calcutta, the chief thoroughfare of the old 'white town'.

Pupu clapped her hands and shrieked, 'What fun! He'd never touch white flesh, it'd disgust him!'

'If he does, he'll have to cleanse himself in the holy Ganga. But how did you learn so much about the dietary norms of tigers, Didi?'

'*Each morning, after Father's drunk his tea, I give the tiger
the dregs left in the cup*'

Pupu-didi smiled sagely. 'I know everything.'

'And I don't, I suppose?'

'Tell me what you know,' challenged Pupu-didi.

'They never touch the flesh of farmers of the kaibarta caste, especially those who live on the western banks of the Ganga. Their scriptures forbid it.'

'And what about those who live on the eastern bank?'

'If they happen to be kaibarta fishermen, their flesh is sacred. Tigers are supposed to eat them by tearing off chunks of flesh with the left paw.'

'Why the left paw?'

'That's the correct ritual. Their pandits maintain that the right paw is dirty. Mind you, Didi, barbers' wives disgust them. You see, barbers' wives paint women's feet red with alta.'[42]

'What's wrong with that?'

'Well, the pandits say that alta is a mere imitation of blood. It isn't real blood drawn by scratching or biting or tearing flesh. Therefore, it's a dishonest thing to put on. They despise such shady dealings. Once, a tiger entered a turban-seller's house. There was a tub of magenta dye in a corner. Mistaking it for blood, he happily plunged his face into it. It was fast dye, if nothing else. The tiger's cheeks and whiskers came up bright red. He went to the densest part of the forest, the region where the tiger-pandits lived. Seeing him, the head tiger, the best mauler among them, exclaimed, 'What on earth! Why's your whole face scarlet?'

'Ashamed, the tiger lied, "I've just polished off a rhino, it must be the blood I've drunk." His lie was found out. The pandit declared, "I don't see a trace of blood on his claws." He sniffed at his mouth and announced he could smell no blood. Everyone

---

[42]*alta*: a red dye used by women to paint their feet.

chorused, "How disgraceful! This is neither blood nor bile nor brain nor marrow—he must have gone to some human settlement and drunk unholy *vegetarian* blood." A committee debated the issue. The biting expert among the tigers roared, "He must perform a penance!" And so he did.'

'What if he had refused?'

'Oh, that would have been a disaster! He has five daughters, all keen-clawed and of marriageable age. Even if he tucked his tail beneath his belly, and offered a dowry of twenty-eight buffaloes, do you think he'd ever find them suitors? And then there would be an even greater punishment.'

'What's that?'

'When he died, no priest would agree to perform the funeral rites. In the end, perhaps, they'd have to call in a wolf-priest from the cane jungles. That would be a terrible disgrace, seven generations of descendants would be unable to hold up their heads for shame.'

'Why have a funeral at all?'

'Just listen to that! Why, his ghost would starve to death.'

'But he's already dead, how could he die again?'

'It's even worse, you see! Death by starvation is permissible, but starvation after death is a fearful calamity.'

This cast Pupu-didi into deep thought. After a while, she asked, frowning, 'In that case, what does an Englishman's ghost eat?'

'What he ate while alive lasts him seven lives. But our bellies start rumbling long before we've even crossed the Baitarani[43] at the mouth of the underworld.'

This doubt cleared, Pupu-didi immediately asked, 'What sort of penance did he have to perform?'

---

[43]*Baitarani*: the river dead souls cross to enter the underworld.

'A tiger learned in the rites of roaring and other tigerish customs decreed he would have to remain in the south-west corner of the square where the shrine of the tiger-goddess stands, from the beginning of the dark lunar fortnight to the middle of the moonless night of Amavasya, feeding only on a shoulder of jackal. Furthermore, the kill could be made by none other than his paternal aunt's daughter or the second son of his wife's maternal cousin. Even worse, the tiger could only use his right hind-paw to tear off the flesh. When he heard this awful sentence passed, the tiger's insides churned. Clasping his four paws in entreaty, he began to howl piteously.'

'Why, what was so awful about it?'

'Good heavens, jackal's meat! It's as profane as meat can be! The tiger swore never to repeat his crime. He whimpered, "Feed me a mongoose's tail, if you will, but not a shoulder of jackal flesh!"'

'Did he have to eat it in the end?'

'Oh yes.'

'Dadamashai, tigers must be very orthodox in matters of religion!'

'Certainly. Do you think they'd abide by as many rules if they weren't? That's why jackals hold them in such respect. If they find a tiger's half-eaten prasad, it becomes a family heirloom! If the thirteenth day of the month of Magh[44] happens to be a Tuesday, many jackals make a pilgrimage to lick the feet of an old tiger in the depths of the night. They believe this wins them religious merit. Innumerable jackals have laid down their lives in the effort.'

---

[44] *Magh*: the tenth month in the Bengali calendar (mid-January to mid-February).

Clasping his four paws in entreaty, he began to howl piteously

Pupu-didi found this hard to swallow. 'If tigers are so very religious, how can they bring themselves to kill for meat? And eat it raw, for that matter?'

'Oh, that's not just any old meat. It's been sanctified by chanting mantras.'

'What kind of mantras?'

'Their very holy snarl-spell. They utter it before they make each kill. You couldn't call that killing, could you?'

'And what if they forget to chant the spell?'

'The most revered tiger-pandit maintains that if a tiger forgets to chant the spell before it makes a kill, it'll be reborn as the beast it has killed. All the tigers are scared stiff of being reborn as humans.'

'Why?'

'In their opinion, the human body is entirely bald, and quite grotesque. Men can't even boast of tails! They need wives just to whisk the flies off their backs. They look like clowns, toddling about on two legs—the sight makes the tigers laugh till they cry. The most renowned contemporary tiger-expert on the history and habits of his race says that when Lord Vishwakarma[45] had nearly finished making the world and was running low on materials, he felt a sudden urge to create humans. Let alone paws, he couldn't even muster a few hooves for the poor creatures—they hide the shame of their naked feet with shoes and of their bodies with clothes. Humankind is the only form of life that suffers from embarrassment. No other creature on earth feels such shame.'

'Tigers must be very haughty creatures.'

---

[45]*Lord Vishwakarma*: the craftsman among the Hindu gods. The Vedas say Vishwakarma created the universe.

'Oh, they are. That's why they're so anxious to preserve their caste. Why, a human girl once put a tiger quite off its food by hinting it would lose caste if it ate her. Our He has composed a poem about it.'

'I'm sure He can't write poems like you do.'

'Well, he thinks he can, and it's not a case you can call in the police to solve.'

'Let's hear it.'

'All right.'

A black-striped tiger, huge and hulking,
Into a mansion one day skulking
After a footman—O toothsome delight!—
Encountered a mirror, and got quite a fright.

The footman fled in a single bound
And the beast in the mirror his own image found.
His fur stood on end; he shouted, 'Alack!
My body is branded with stripes of black!'

With the rice-paddle Putu stood husking some rice:
The tiger arrived at the spot in a trice.
He puffed out his whiskers (his only hope!)
And fiercely demanded some glycerine soap.

Putu was puzzled. 'Now what was that word?
It isn't one I can claim to have heard.
Of high-flown learning I've suffered a dearth,
The sad result of my lowly birth.'

'Lies!' the tiger exclaimed with a scowl.
'D'you think I'm blind?' he began to growl.
'The glycerine soap must be all-effacing:
'What else could remove the stripes from your casing?'

Putu was vexed. 'I'm dark!' she moped.
Nobody's seen me glycerine-soap'd.
You're joking: I'm not a memsahib's aunt.
Supply you with soap, therefore, I can't.'

'Aren't you ashamed?' hear the tiger shout.
'I'll crunch up your bones and your flesh, you lout!'

Putu exclaimed, 'You shameless old sinner!
You're doomed if you try to devour me for dinner!
Of humble caste am I, don't you know?
Mahatma Gandhi loves my tribe so![46]
Calm down, don't lose your temper, I pray.'

Yelled the tiger in fright, 'Don't touch me, I say!
Oh, fie upon me! Oh, woe and disgrace!
In Tiger-Town what scorn I'll face!
My name will be sunk; full of daughters my house—
Not one of the girls will find her a spouse.
The Tiger-Goddess will with curses assail me:
No glycerine soap—I'm off to bewail me!

'You know, Pupu-didi, there's a great to-do among the tigers now in the name of progress. The speakers for the movement are going around telling everyone that rejecting certain kinds of flesh as profane is disrespectful to the blessed spirit of the dead animal. They declare, "From now on, we'll eat whatever we can kill; we'll eat with both right paw and left paw, fore-paw and hind-paw; we'll eat whether we've chanted the snarl-spell or not." They've gone to the extent of resolving to claw their prey

---

[46]Mahatma Gandhi protested against caste-based social injustice and worked for the uplift of the so-called lower castes and untouchables.

on Thursdays and bite it on Saturdays—such enlightened emancipation! These tigers are great ones for arguments, and make a great show of respect for all forms of life. They're so noble-minded that they want to eat even the kaibarta farmers on the west bank of the Ganga. They've got into a huge row about all this. The puritan tigers have dubbed them "Kaibarta-Clawers". They've come in for a lot of chaffing, as a result.'

Pupe asked, 'Dadamashai, have you ever written a poem about tigers?'

Loath to admit defeat, I said I had.

'Do let me hear it.'

Gravely, I began to recite:

O God our Maker, you have not belittled might,
But with powerful hand bestowed it as right
In him that is strongest—amazing your grace!
An awesome predator, keen-clawed, with face
As fearsome as comely; a frame like a streak
Of lightning—crashing down to wreak
Splendid havoc—Lord Shiva's passion[47]
Rages in the creature you have fashioned.
The storm unstemmed by creation's decree,
Reared hood of froth in the foaming sea,
The raging lion that your mercy defies,
The awful thunder of giants' war cries,
The tongues of hungry fire that dart
Through rock and soil, to brand the heart
Of the stormy sky, and the drunken flood
Cruel, unashamed, revolt in its blood—

---

[47]*Lord Shiva's passion*: destructive frenzy. Shiva is the god of destruction.

All these are rebels, immortal, unbroken:
Through them the voice of terror has spoken.
Your creature belongs to this awesome race:
No power dares mock his terrible grace.

Pupu was silent. 'Well, Didi?' I asked. 'You didn't seem to like it.'

Abashed, she replied, 'No, no, of course I liked it. It's just that I can't quite find a tiger in it.'

'Where else should he be but hiding in the bushes? You can't see him, but he's there all the same, all the more terrible because he's hidden.'

'You told me about the glycerine-seeking tiger long ago,' mused Pupu. 'How did He come to hear of him?'

'He steals all my stories and puts them on his own lips.'

'But—'

'"But" just about sums it up. Not that he made too bad a job of the poem.'

'But—'

'Quite correct. I don't write that way, perhaps I can't. But this isn't the first time he's pinched my material and polished it up a bit. Once that's done, it's hard to recognize again. Take that other rhyme of his—very like the first one—'

'I want to hear it.'

'Very well, listen:

There lived a fat tiger, the forest his home.
Day after day
In search of prey
His stripy frame would roam.
But he'd throw a fit
If he chanced to hit

With whisker-puffing heat
Upon the fact
His dinner lacked
A pound or two of meat.

One day he snarled
At Baturam gnarled
And bald as a pink-faced baby,
'Go wake your wife:
Ten lambs or your life!
Lay the table, you gormless old gaby!'

Cried Batu, 'What's this?
There's much that's amiss
In your manners as well as your breeding.
It's late at night,
But you'll pick a fight
Whenever your tum needs feeding!

'You chose to stumble
Upon my hearth humble—
But think of the tigress you've wed!
Into space she scowls
While her stomach growls,
But she'll only eat when you're fed.

'At home you've stored
The iguana you gored,
And the shrivelled corpse of a toad,
A rabbit stale
With a stink to regale—
It's waiting for you down the road.

'Or else you'll find that the papers
Are raising Cain over your capers—'

'Oh Lord Almighty!
Your talk is too flighty
My head's in a whirl with your scolding.
My brain's all a-clatter
With your foolish chatter,
But meanwhile, my meal you're withholding!

'Your hairless pate
Will meet a grim fate
Unless you come out and drop guard.
To save your skin
You must give in,
And show me the goats in your yard.'

Then Baturam swore
To fall at the four
Huge feet of the stripy old glutton,
But said, 'It's a sin
To do someone in,
And worse to steal all his mutton!'

The tiger said,
'What if I die instead?
That'll rouse the Creator's ire!
And then my missus
Deprived of my kisses
Will die on my funeral pyre.

'So out with my meat,
Or it's you that I'll eat.'—
He raised his paw for a clout.
Batu said in a flap,
'Don't be hasty, old chap:
Let's see if my goats are about.'

The tiger was led
By his host to a shed.

Batu said, 'Here endeth your quest!'
He did not hesitate
To fasten the gate
And bar it upon his guest.

Then wondered the beast,
'I don't see my feast—
Can it be that Batu is cheating?
There's nor hide nor hair
Of my promised fare,
Nor sound of its agonized bleating.

'Batu seems bent
With savage intent
On having a fellow-beast die.
I'll collar the hound,
Pin him to the ground
And suck out his blood till he's dry.

This filthy shed—'
'It's for coal,' Batu said.
'It was once the dairyman's nest.
The God of the Dead
Now sleeps here instead,
And he'll guide your soul unto rest.'

The tiger puffed out his whiskers:
'What's become of the bleating friskers?'

Said Batu in glee,
'They're all within me!
Go search the whole town if you must,
You won't find a trace
Of them in the place—
I've crunched all their bones into dust!'

'Did you like it?'

'Whatever you might say, Dadamashai, I think He writes beautiful tiger-poems.'

I replied, 'Well, that's as it may be. But wait another ten years before you venture to judge whether he writes better than I do.'

'When I open the window, he giggles'

Pupu changed the subject. 'But my tiger doesn't come to eat me.'

'Since I can see you right before me, I should say he doesn't. What *does* your tiger do?'

'At night, when I'm in bed, he comes and scratches at the windowpane. When I open it, he giggles.'

'That's perfectly possible. Tigers are great ones for laughing— what they call "humorous" in English. They bare their gums at the slightest provocation.'

7

PUPU CAME TO ME AND ASKED, 'DADAMASHAI, DIDN'T YOU SAY YOU'D invited He here on Saturday? What happened?'

'It went off very well. Haji Mian had made some of his sheekh kebabs—delicious!'

'And then?'

'And then I ate three-quarters of them, and gave that urchin Kalu the rest. Kalu said, "Dada, this tastes better than our plantain dumplings!"'

'Didn't He eat anything?'

'He didn't have a chance.'

'Didn't he even come?'

'How could he?'

'Well then, where is he?'

'Nowhere.'

'At home?'

'No.'

'Gone back to his village?'

'No.'

'Abroad, then?'

'No.'

'You told me it was almost arranged that He should go to the Andaman Islands. Is that where he's gone?'

'He didn't need to go.'

'Then why aren't you telling me what's actually happened?'

'Because you'll be either frightened or grieved.'
'I don't care. You'll have to tell me what's happened.'
'Very well then, listen—'

The other day, having a class to teach, I was supposed to read the learned text *Bidagdhamukhamandan*.[48] After a while, I suddenly discovered that *The History of Panchu Pakrashi's Aunt-in-Law* had found its way into my hands. I must have dozed off as I read; it was then half past two in the morning. I dreamt that our cook Kini had had her face badly burnt when some boiling oil blazed into flame. Having performed penance for seven days and seven nights, she was granted two tins of Lahiri's Moonlight Snow. She scoured her face with it, but I told her, 'That won't do any good; go get some skin from the cheek of a buffalo-calf and have it sewn on your face—nothing else will match your complexion.' The words were scarcely out of my mouth when she borrowed three and a quarter rupees from me and rushed off to Dharmatala market to buy a calf. At this point, I heard a strange whooshing noise in the room. It sounded as if someone was dragging his feet, clad in shoes of wind, all over the floor. I started up and hurriedly turned up the flame of my lantern. It was clear there was someone in the room, but I couldn't make out who or what it was, or even what it looked like. My heart was thudding, but I called out as sternly as I could, 'Who are you? Shall I call the police?'

The intruder replied in strange hoarse tones, 'Now then,

[48]Bidagdhamukhamandan: *Ornament of the Learned Countenance*, a twelfth-century Buddhist text by Dharmadas. The jokes lies in an alternative meaning of *bidagdhamukha*, 'burnt face'.

Dada, don't you recognize me? I'm your Pupu-didi's He! Don
you remember inviting me here?'

'Don't talk nonsense,' I retorted. 'You look like nothing o
earth!'

'That's just it, you see,' he answered. 'I've lost my body.'

'Lost it? What do you mean?'

'You look like nothing on earth!'

'I'll tell you what I mean. Knowing I was invited to a feast at Pupu-didi's, I went off to bathe bright and early. It was just half past one in the afternoon. Sitting on the steps of Telenipara Ghat, I was scrubbing vigorously at my face with a pumice stone. It was so soothing that, before I knew it, I was lost to the world in a comfortable drowse. I slumped right over and fell headlong into the water. I don't know what happened after that. I couldn't tell if I was on dry land, or still in the water. All I knew was that I wasn't there any more.'

'Not there!'

'I swear on your life—'

'You needn't bother about my life, just go on.'

'I was itching and tried to scratch myself, but couldn't find the itchy place nor the fingernails to scratch it with. I felt so miserable that I began to blubber. But even the blubbering that I had enjoyed freely since childhood failed me now. The louder I howled, the less it sounded as if I were howling: you couldn't hear a single wail. I wanted to knock my head against the old banyan tree, but I couldn't even find my holy hair-tuft. But my most painful experience was wandering about by the poolside, even as the clock struck twelve, crying, "Where's my hunger? Where's my hunger?" But that monkey of an appetite evaded me entirely.'

'I can't make head or tail of your story. Stop a minute.'

'I beg of you, Dada, don't ask me to stop. An unstopped being like you can never imagine the agony of being stopped. I won't stop, I won't stop, I'll go on for as long as I possibly can!'

So saying, he began to caper around the room, making a series of loud thuds and winding up with a display of the most astonishing gymnastics on my carpet. His antics reminded me of the gambols of a happy porpoise.

'I slumped right over and fell headlong into the water'

'What do you think you're doing?'

'Dada, after that royal finale of mine, you'll never find me stopping again. I'll be pleased if you resort to violence. When I discovered the absence of a back worthy of a few sound blows, I remembered my old teacher Satkari and felt as if my heart would burst with agony—only I didn't have a heart either. If such a fate were to befall a carp, it would implore the cook to toss it into a cauldron of boiling oil and fry it to a crisp. Ah me, that back I've now lost—the number of cuffs my old teacher showered on it! I swallowed them like sweetmeats made of brick. Today, it seems as if—oh, Dada, do pummel my back just once, as hard as you can—'

He came over and presented his back to me.

'Go away!' I shrieked.

'Let me finish,' said He. 'I traipsed from village to village, searching high and low for a body. It was about three o'clock in the afternoon. The hotter the sun grew, the less it bothered me. My misery was almost complete, when I came upon old Uncle Patu, who had been smoking ganja in the shade of a banyan tree, and had fallen fast asleep. I seemed to see the life within him gather itself into a single, vital point and rise pulsing to the very crown of his head. I saw a golden opportunity before me. Without the slightest hesitation, I squeezed my invisible spirit through the nostrils of his inert form, just as one might thrust one's feet into a new pair of nagra shoes. Patu's inner man wheezed to life.

'"Now, who might you be, son? There's no room for you in here."

'By then, I had seized his voice. "It's you there isn't any room for," I retorted. "Out you go!"

Patu's missus

'He gasped, "I'm on my way; there's just a little bit of me left inside. Push."

'I gave him a hefty shove, and he disappeared with a whoosh.

'Meanwhile, Patu's missus had arrived on the scene. "There you are, you old good-for-nothing!"

'Her scolding was music to my ears. "Do say that once more," I pleaded. "I never thought I'd hear such a yell again."

'The old dame thought I was playing the fool; she disappeared into the house in search of a broom. The fear of losing my newly gleaned body gripped me. I thought it best to go home. When I looked in the mirror, a shudder passed through me. I felt like paring the skin from my face with a carpenter's plane.

'The bodyless had found a body all right, but his original appearance was still sunk seven fathoms deep in the lake; how could it be recovered?

'Just at this point, after a painful separation, I was reunited with my appetite. My hunger returned in a rush. It gnawed at every fibre of my stomach. I could hardly see from emptiness. It was one of those cases of "first encountered, first eaten". What bliss!

'I remembered I was invited to a meal at Pupu-didi's. I didn't have the money for the train fare, so I set out on foot. The very effort of walking was such an unimaginable comfort. My ecstasy soon had me drenched in perspiration. I took one step after another, and chanted to myself, "I'm not stopping, I'm not stopping, I'm going on and on." I've never walked with such verve in my life. Dada, you've got an entire body ensconced in that armchair of yours—you don't know the happiness of tiring yourself out. The ache in your bones tells you you're alive, and with a vengeance—beyond all doubt or question.'

'I see, I see, but do tell me what you want to do now.'

'The duty of doing something rests entirely with you, Dada. You're the host, it won't do if you forget to feed your guest.'

'Neither will it do if you forget that it's three o'clock in the morning.'

'Then I'm off to visit Pupu-didi!'

'Don't you dare!'

'Dada, it's no use threatening me any more, you've done your worst. I'm off!'

'On no account.'

'I *shall* go,' he insisted.

To which I replied, 'I'd like to see you do it!'

He began chanting, 'I shall, I shall, I shall!'

He climbed onto my table and began to dance up and down on it. 'I shall go, I shall go!'

In the end, he struck up a song to the tune of a panchali:[49] 'I shall, I shall, I shall!'

I couldn't stand it any longer. I grabbed the end of his long hair-tuft and tugged hard. Without a word of warning, his body slithered off him like a loose sock and fell to the ground with a thump.

What a disaster! How was I to communicate with the spirit of this ganja-fuddled dodderer? I screeched into the night, 'Hey, listen, come back, get into this body of yours and take it away!'

Not a sound in reply. I'm thinking of putting out an advertisement in the *Anandabazar Patrika*.[50]

'Is all this true, Dadamashai?' asked Pupu-didi, round-eyed.

'It's much more than the truth, Didi,' I replied. 'It's a story.'

---

[49] *panchali*: a kind of traditional song.

[50] Anandabazar Patrika: a Bengali newspaper, in wide circulation to this day.

8

I WAS PREPARING SOME NOTES ON THE *AREOPAGITICA*[51] FOR AN MA CLASS.
For this I needed to consult a book—*The International Mellifluous Abracadabra* and also had to slit open the pages of *Three Hundred Years of Indo-Indetermination*, to look things up in its Appendix. I had asked the library to get me a copy of *The Onomatopoeia of Tintinnabulation*. All of a sudden, He burst headlong into the room.

'What's the matter?' I inquired. 'Has your wife hanged herself?'

He answered, 'She certainly would have, had she existed. What a to-do you've made!'

'Why, what's the matter?'

'Till now, you've made up scores of absurd stories about me. Thank heavens you haven't referred to me by name, otherwise I'd have found it hard to hold up my head in polite society. But I knew they amused Pupu-didi, so I suffered them in silence. But now, it's just the opposite!'

'Why don't you tell me what's really happened?'

'Then listen. Yesterday, Pupu-didi had gone to the cinema. She was about to get into the car, when I came up from behind her and said, "Pupu-didi, take me with you in your car." And after that—I can't describe to you, Dada, the panic that ensued. Sheer hysteria.'

---

[51] Areopagitica: a famous prose treatise by Milton on the freedom of writing and publication.

'What was it like?'

'Pupu-didi covered her eyes with her hands and screamed, "Go away, you can't get into my car after stealing a body from that ganja-addict!" People came running from all directions; the police almost marched me off to jail. I've been faced with many insults, Dada, but never one as original as this. Stealing the body of a ganja-addict! Not even my best friend has ever slandered me so infamously. I went home and heard the whole story. It must be your doing.'

'Of course it's my doing. What else could I have done? How long can I go on making up these tales about you? I'm not getting any younger; my pen seems to have developed a touch of rheumatism. It's lost that happy lightness needed to concoct impossible tales about you that might appeal to Pupu-didi's tastes. So I thought to finish you off once and for all in that last story.'

'But I'm not ready to be finished off, Dada. I beg of you, do ease Pupu-didi's fears. Tell her it was only a story.'

'I did try, but it isn't easy to pacify her. The fear has twisted itself around her nerves. I went to the extent of bringing that old ganja-smoker Patu before her, but it had exactly the opposite effect of what I'd hoped for. She took it as clear evidence that you were wandering about in Patu's skin.'

'In that case, Dada, I suggest you turn the story around. Let Patu die of tetanus, and cremate his body at Nimtala Ghat.[52] We'll stage an elaborate funeral and invite Pupu-didi to it. I'll pay whatever it costs from my own pocket. I'm the juggler, the shape-shifter in Pupu-didi's stories—it'll kill me to be ousted from a position of such importance.'

---

[52]*Nimtala Ghat*: a cremation ground in Calcutta.

'All right, we'll turn the procession of chariots around and take you back to Pupu-didi's home.'

He came the next evening, and I began the story.

'Patu's wife has filed a lawsuit against you, to establish her claims on her husband,' I said.

He interrupted before I could get any further. 'That won't do at all, Dada,' he protested. 'You've never met Patu's missus. If that lady happens to win the case, the defendant will have to take to opium and kill himself.'

'Don't worry. Whether she wins or loses, I promise I'll have you last your course.'

'Very well, go on.'

'You joined your palms in supplication and pleaded, "My lord, defender of the law, I swear by seven generations of my ancestors, I'm not her husband."'

'The prosecutor glared at you. "What do you mean by saying you're not her husband?" he demanded.

'"I just mean that to this date I have not married her. Try as I might, I can't immediately think of any second meaning."

'Ramsaday, the prosecutor, scolded you roundly. "Of course you're her husband. Don't you lie to us!"

'You turned to the judge. "I've told plenty of lies in my life, but to lie that I married this old harridan of my own accord, while of sound mind and body, would take more nerve than I possess. The mere idea makes my heart quake."

'Then they interrogated thirty-five ganja-fuddled witnesses. One by one, they ran their fingers, blackened with packing the ganja into the bowls of their pipes, over your face and said, "It looks exactly like Patu, down to the lump on the forehead. But——"

Ramsaday, the prosecutor

"'But what?' demanded the prosecutor angrily.

"'It's Patu to the life, but how can we swear it actually *is* Patu? We knew his wife; our friend suffered not a little at her hands. The number of brooms smashed to bits over his luckless shoulders! If we could have saved the price of those, we wouldn't have had to scrimp and pinch when it came to ganja. You see, sir, that's why we can't take an oath in court that would bring disaster upon a gentleman."

'The prosecutor scowled furiously. "Then who is this man? Not even God Almighty could summon the nerve to build another Patu!"

'The chief of the ganja-addicts countered, "You're right, son. Such a creation could have evolved only once, by accident. After that first time, God rubbed his nose in contrition and vowed never to make such a mistake again. But it's obvious that some devil wanted to get back at him. It's a masterly fake—the work of an expert. As Patu's body shrivelled, his nose grew hooked and pinched. You'd think it was that very crescent moon of a nose that had been grafted on to this face. A thousand little bats must have sacrificed their wings to craft the skin on his hands."

'You saw the trial heading for disaster and hastened to seek out the judge. "Give me a week's time, and I'll have the mythical Patu before you in the flesh."

'You rushed back to Telenipara Ghat. Luckily, your own body bobbed to the surface just in that instant. You stretched Patu's body carefully out on the ground and reoccupied your own. Heaving an immense sigh of relief, you turned your face up to the heavens and shouted, "Hey, Patu!"

'His cast-off form got to its feet. Patu said, "Brother, I was with you all this time. The ganja made me light-headed and restless. I wanted to finish myself off, but you stood in my way. When I was alive, I had a decided taste for life. As soon as I'd died, the misery of never being able to die again overwhelmed me. I wasn't even fit to put a rope round my neck."

'"Well, we've done what we had to do," you said. "Now come along to court with me. I'll have the judge arrange for an allowance of ganja to be doled out to you."

'The two of you went back to court. The judge scolded Patu, "Is this old woman your wife or not?"

'Patu answered, "Sir, my instincts bid me deny it. But I'm a gentleman; why should I commit the sin of lying? I know she'll catch up with me sooner or later—like the rest of my sins. She is, I own, my first partner in matrimony."

'"Are there others?" inquired the judge.

'Patu replied, 'I have to have a few more, for the sake of appearances. I'm a kulin[53] by birth. Pure kulin blood!"

Pupu-didi read the story on Sunday. She asked, 'Dadamashai, you've said you were writing some college text, and looking at lots and lots of English books. But you don't have a college! Besides, I've never seen you open one of those books you talked about. All you write are rhymes!'

I avoided giving her a direct answer. Instead, I smiled a little smile.

'Dadamashai, do you know Sanskrit?'

'Now look here, Pupu-didi, such questions are very indelicate. You should never ask them to one's face.'

---

[53]*kulin*: a Brahmin of pure, unsullied caste. They exploited this status to indulge in polygamy.

9

PUPU-DIDI APPEARED SOMEWHAT PERTURBED IN THE MORNING. 'Dadamashai, have you run out of stories about He?'

Dadamashai abandoned his newspaper and pushed his glasses up his forehead. 'It's not the stories' but the storyteller's days that are numbered.'

'He got his body back, didn't he? Do tell me what's going to happen now.'

'Well, he'll have to go back to earning his bread by the sweat of his brow. Often, he'll have to come forward and shoulder lots of responsibilities. At other times, he'll shrug them off. Sometimes he'll take his work very seriously and puzzle his head over it. At other times, he'll put his feet up on the desk. Perhaps people will be annoyed by his laziness and say he doesn't set his mind to anything. His head will swim on occasion, and his stomach churn. His limbs will be overcome by languor and refuse to get out of bed. His body will feel slow and heavy at times— at others, shudders will run up and down his spine. Sometimes he'll look upon the world with a benevolent eye, and sometimes it'll make his blood rise. Some people will say things that make his ears tingle, others things to calm his fraught nerves. His hands will grow clammy at some of the things his friends talk about. Such a lot of complications—all rooted in some part or other of that body of his.'

'Dadamashai, when he was roaming about in someone else's

body, which of them suffered all these problems? When his head buzzed and his insides churned, did he feel it, or did Patu?'

'That's a very difficult question you've asked. I don't know, and if you ask him, I'm sure it'll make the poor fellow's head swim.'

'Dadamashai, I never thought one's body could cause one so many problems.'

'It's by stringing all those problems together that you make a story. Why, the story sits astride the body, like a hunter on his horse, and goes racing in all directions, as far as the eye can see. Some bodies serve for stories as asses do, others as the royal elephant in an imperial procession.'

'What's your body like, Dadamashai?'

'I won't tell you. The scriptures condemn vanity.'

'Dadamashai, why did you stop telling me stories about He?'

'Let me explain. Idleness is the highest state of heavenly bliss. The Indra[54] who reigns above, luxuriously sipping nectar, with his thousand eyelids drooping, is the God of Storytelling. I used to worship him once, but now I find myself unable even to enter his courts. I've stopped receiving my share of the holy food of fiction.'

'Why?'

'I once forgot the way.'

'How?'

The heavenly river Suradhuni that flows through the celestial city of Amaravati cradles the abode of the gods. But its ebb tide reveals another heaven. Dense black smoke from factory chimneys billows like a flag in the sky. That's the Paradise of Labour. Lord

---

[54]*Indra*: king of the Hindu gods.

Vishwakarma presides there, resplendent in workers' shorts. One autumn morning, I was walking along the street carrying a plate of sheuli flowers for morning worship, when a priest's agent descended upon me on a bicycle. His satchel was bulging with notebooks, and I could see two fountain pens—one with red ink in it, the other with black—sticking out of his pocket. Bundles of newspaper clippings sprouted from the pockets of his China-coat. The watch on his right wrist was set to Standard Time, the one on his left to Calcutta Time. His bag was stuffed with railway timetables, for the EIR and EBR, ABR and NWR, BNR, BBR and SIR.[55] In his breast pocket was a notebook-cum-diary.

'What hell-pit are you off to today, with your face turned up to the heavens?' he demanded of me.

'Don't be angry, Panda-ji,' I pleaded. 'I'm going to offer prayers in the temple, but I can't find the way.'

'I suppose you're one of that head-in-the-air, can't-find-the-way crew?' he scolded. 'Come on, I'll show you the way.'

He dragged me off to the temple of Lord Vishwakarma. I was given no chance to protest. Before I could open my mouth, he commanded, 'Put down that plate of flowers here and fork out your offering. Five quarter-rupees.'

I performed the puja like an idiot. He immediately copied down the accounts in his notebook. Then he glanced at one of his wristwatches and declared, 'All right, your work's done. I don't have much time now. Scoot!'

From the very next day, I began to notice the fruit of my devotions. It was half past four in the morning. I woke up with a

---

[55]*EIR...*: abbreviations of the names of various railway systems in British India.

start, thinking robbers had broken in. But it was only the Society
for the Protection of Orphans. The members had rounded up
twenty-five boys, all between the ages of twelve and thirteen,
who were standing at the door, singing loudly:

> Your stomachs you stuff
>   With more than enough,
> In your pockets you stash
>   Your bundles of cash,
> But add up the due,
>   You'll find that it's true
> That of your reserve,
>   The orphans deserve
> The larger share,
>   And love and fond care.
> So arise and awake
>   For the orphans' sake.
>   O, give to the poor; help lessen their pain—
>   O, give to the poor and give once again!

Yelling this refrain, they gave the khol[56] a number of tremendous
whacks. The more I tried to reckon in my head how much money
I had left, the more fiercely the beat assaulted my ears. Someone
picked up the rhythm with a pair of castanets, and the boys struck
up a jig. The din grew unbearable. I unlocked the safe and took
out my money-bag. Their leader, sporting a week-old stubble,
eagerly stretched out a sheet down below. On being shaken, the
bag yielded exactly one rupee, nine annas and three paise. The
month was all but over, and I had only just managed to save this
money to pay the tailor's bill.

---

[56]*khol*: a kind of drum played at both ends.

'O, give to the poor and give once again!'

The music gave way to abuse. 'Sitting pretty on your pots
of money, with your feet up on a feather bed!' they yelled.
'Remember this, the day you die, you millionaires will be worth
no more than us beggars in our rags!'

The harangue was old stuff, but being called a millionaire
sent a spasm of rage through me.

That was just the beginning. Since then, I've been elected to
no less than twenty-five committees. I've become the certified
president of all societies in Bengal: the Society for the Revival
of Ancient Indian Music, the Society for Eradication of the Pond-
Choking Water Hyacinth, the Society for the Cremation of the
Dead, the Society for the Improvement of Literature, the Society
for the Unification of the Three Poets Chandidas,[57] the Society
for the Reform of Trade in Sugar-cane Fibres, the Society for the
Reclamation of Khana's Lost Homestead at Khanyan,[58] the
Society for the Improvement of Conditions in Homes for Aged
Cattle, the Society for the Protection of Whiskers and Reduction
of Barber's Bills—I have become a distinguished member of all
these. I have been requested to write a preface to a treatise on
tetanus, to pronounce my opinion on modern mathematical
textbooks, to bestow my blessings upon the book *The Identification
of Bhavabhuti's Birthplace at Bhubandanga*,[59] to find a name for the

---

[57] *Three Poets Chandidas*: There are thought to be several medieval Bengali poets
sharing this famous name.

[58] *Khana's Lost Homestead at Khanyan*: Khana was a legendary woman of learning,
the supposed composer of couplets of traditional wisdom. Fancifully linked
here, because of the similarity of sound, with Khanyan, a place north of
Calcutta in Hooghly district of West Bengal.

[59] *Bhavabhuti's Birthplace at Bhubandanga*: Bhavabhuti, an ancient Sanskrit
poet, alliteratively linked in the same way to Bhubandanga, a locality near
Shantiniketan.

infant daughter of the forest officer at Rawalpindi, to sing the praises of a particular brand of shaving soap,[60] and to recount my personal experience of medicines for lunatics.

'Dadamashai, you talk so much nonsense for no reason at all that no one ever believes you when you say you don't have the time for something. Today you simply have to tell me what He did when he got his body back.'

'He was immensely pleased and rushed off to Dumdum.'

'Dumdum!'

'You see, our He has got his ears back after quite a while. Now he just can't get over his urge to hear every bit of sound for himself. He pricks up his ears at Shyambazar crossing: he delights in the rumble of buses and trams. He's befriended the guard at the Titagarh jute mill, who lets him sit in his room for hours on end, listening to the grinding of the machines. The noise almost lulls him to sleep. He takes a snack of aloo dum and rosogollas with him in a paper bag, to eat at the workshop of the Baron Company's blacksmith. The British troops have marched to Dumdum for target practice. It was the booming of their guns that he was listening to, sitting comfortably behind the targets. Unable to restrain his excitement, he poked out his face, caught a bullet in the head—and that was it.'

'That was what, Dadamashai?'

'That was that—meaning all my stories about him are quite finished.'

'No, no, that simply can't happen. You're trying to dodge me. All the stories in the world could end that way.'

'And so they do.'

'Not this story. What happened after that?'

---

[60]*shaving soap*: The joke lies in the fact that Rabindranath had a flowing beard.

'After he was dead? You can't be serious.'

'Yes, after he was dead.'

'I see you've become quite the Savitri[61] of myth.'

.'No, you can't fob me off with all that. Tell me what happened next.'

'Very well. They say that once you're dead, nothing can hurt you. Let me prove to you that even when you're dead, you're not safe. The army surgeon, a famous man, was in his tent. When he heard that the poor fellow was dead of a bullet in the skull, he leapt up and let out a joyful "Hurrah!"'

'Why was he pleased?'

'He said, "Now we can experiment with a brain transplant."'

'How can you transplant a brain?'

'It's a feat of science. He sent for a gorilla from the zoo, and extracted its brain. Then he cranked open our man's skull, put in the gorilla's grey matter and kept the head bound up in plaster of lime for fifteen days. The skull became whole once again. But when our He got off his bed—what a nightmare! He bared his teeth at anyone he saw and chattered excitedly. The nurse took to her heels. The great doctor seized his patient's hands in an iron grip and thundered, 'Now sit here quietly and behave yourself!' He understood the bellow, but not the language. He didn't want to sit on the couch: he was determined to jump onto the table. But he couldn't manage the leap, and fell on the floor with a bump. The door was open; there was an ashvatthva tree outside. Dodging all his captors, he made a bolt for the

---

[61]*Savitri*: She successfully pleaded with Yama, the God of Death, to restore her husband, Satyavana, to life.

tree. He imagined he'd be among the branches in a single bound. He kept making wild springs at it, and falling down heavily each time he tried. His failure bewildered him. He began working himself into a rage. His frantic leaps sent the boys of the medical college into gales of mirth. He kept baring his teeth and making little rushes at them. One of the Anglo-Indian students was sitting under a tree with his legs stretched out, enjoying a snack of bread and butter with bananas, laid out neatly on a napkin. Our He pounced on the unsuspecting fellow and snatched away his fruit. The youth lost his temper and tried to hit him. Meanwhile, his friends couldn't stop their guffaws.

There was great consternation when it came to deciding who should take charge of him. Some were all for sending him to the zoo, others advised the orphanage. The zookeeper objected, 'We can't keep humans here.' The superintendent of the orphanage demurred, 'Our rules won't allow a monkey to be kept here.'

'Dadamashai, why did you stop?'

'Didimani, at the absolute end of absolutely everything in this world of ours, there comes a stop.'

'No, this can't have stopped yet. Anybody could snatch a banana and eat it.'

'I'll tell you the rest tomorrow. I have work to do today.'

'Do tell me what's going to happen tomorrow. Just a little bit.'

'You know our He has received a proposal of marriage, don't you? Well, the bride's family haven't heard that his brain's been exchanged. They've settled the day and hour of the wedding. The groom's uncle cooled him down with two enormous bunches of bananas, and led him to the venue for the wedding.

And after that—when I describe to you the pandemonium that followed, you'll be forced to acknowledge that it's a story indeed. We won't need to kill him off after that. He'll be beyond death.'

It was evening, and I was sitting on the terrace, enjoying the southerly breeze. It was shukla chaturthi, the fourth evening of the bright phase of the moon, and the moon was shining radiantly. Pupu-didi had brought with her a wreath of akanda flowers on a glass platter. After the story, I was to receive my reward.

Meanwhile, He arrived, out of breath. He said, 'Today I'm resigning from my job of finding matter for your stories. I didn't say anything when you dressed me in that ganja-addict Patu's skin. But I can't have you putting an ape's brain in my skull. Who knows what you'll do next? Perhaps you'll turn me into a fruit bat, or a lizard, or a dung beetle. I'd believe you capable of anything. Today, when I sat down in my chair at the office, what did I find on my desk? A bunch of yellow bananas. Normally I'm not averse to a few bananas. But now I see I'll have to give up eating bananas altogether. Pupu-didi, if this grandfather of yours turns me into a Brahmin ogre or a headless spectre next, make sure the tale doesn't get into print. I've already received a visit from my father-in-law-to-be. He'd promised me eighty tolas of gold as his daughter's dowry; now it's come down to thirteen. They know I'll find it difficult to get another bride, after what you've done to my reputation. So now I'm off, and a very good bye to you.'

10

IT WAS EVENING, AND I WAS SITTING IN THE SOUTHERN COURTYARD. THE stars were invisible, hidden behind a screen of venerable rain trees. Alive with fireflies, their branches seemed to wink a hundred jewel-bright eyes at me.

I remarked to Pupu-didi, 'Your wits are ripening rather precociously, so today I think I'll remind you that at one time you too were young.'

Didi laughed. 'You win there. I can't remind you that at one time, you were young as well.'

I sighed. 'Probably no one can any longer. Only the stars in the sky can bear witness to my forgotten childhood. But enough about me—let me tell you a story of your own past childishness. I don't know if you'll enjoy it, but I'll find it sweet.'

'Very well, go on.'

I think it was the month of Phalgun.[62] For the past few days, that Kishori Chatto,[63] with his shiny bald head, had been entertaining you with stories from the *Ramayana*. One morning as I sat reading a newspaper and sipping tea, you arrived, wide-eyed.

I exclaimed, 'What's the matter?'

---

[62]*Phalgun*: the eleventh month of the Bengali year (mid-February to mid-March).
[63]*Kishori Chatto*: an employee of the Tagore household in Rabindranath's own childhood, here imagined as belonging to Pupe's times. Chatto is a short form of the surname Chattopadhyay or Chatterjee.

You gasped, 'I've been kidnapped!'

'Great heavens! Who could have committed this nefarious deed?'

You hadn't yet thought up an answer to that. You could have said it was Ravana,[64] but since that wouldn't have been true, you felt a twinge of misgiving. In the story you'd been told the previous evening, Ravana had been killed in battle—not one of his ten heads had survived. Not seeing a way out, you replied, 'He told me to keep it a secret.'

'Now you've created a problem. How am I to rescue you now? Which way did he take you?'

'Oh, through an unknown country.'

'It wasn't Khandesh, was it?'

'No.'

'Not Bundelkhand?'

'No.'

'What kind of a country was it?'

'It had rivers and mountains and big trees. In some parts it was dark, in others there was light.'

'All that doesn't make it any different from lots of other countries. Did you happen to see anything in the nature of a demon? With spikes, and a tongue hanging out?'

'Yes, yes, he stuck out his tongue at me and disappeared.'

'He does seem to slip through one's fingers. Otherwise, I'd have seized him by the hair-tuft by now. Anyway, he must have borne you off in something. Was it in a chariot?'

'No.'

'On horseback?'

---

[64]*Ravana*: the ten-headed demon-king whom Rama defeated in the *Ramayana*.

With spikes, and a tongue hanging out

'No.'

'On an elephant?'

You blurted out, 'On a rabbit!' Thoughts of this animal had been springing to your mind every now and then of late: your father had given you a pair on your birthday.

I said, 'Well, now we know who the villain is.'

With a mischievous smile, you said, 'Tell me who it is.'

'This, without doubt, is the doing of old Uncle Moon.'

'How did you know?'

'Keeping rabbits is an old habit with him too.'[65]

'Where did he get them?'

'Your father didn't give them to him.'

'Then who did?'

'He slipped into Lord Brahma's zoo[66] and stole them.'

'Shame on him!'

'Shame on him, no question. That's why Lord Brahma stained his body with black, as a punishment.'

'Serve him right.'

'But he doesn't seem to have learnt his lesson. He's gone back to his thieving ways, and actually stolen *you* this time! He probably wants you to feed his rabbits cauliflower leaves with your little hands.'

You were pleased to hear this. To test my cunning, you said, 'Very well, let's see if you know *how* the rabbit carried me off on his back.'

---

[65]In Bengali folk tales, the dark patches on the moon are often said to be in the shape of a rabbit.

[66]*Lord Brahma's zoo*: presumably the entire animal kingdom, which was created by Lord Brahma, creator of the universe.

'You must have been asleep.'

'Do people become lighter when they sleep?'

'Of course. Haven't you ever flown in your sleep?'

'Yes, I've flown all right.'

'Then where's the problem? Why, it's easy for a rabbit. A mere bullfrog could hoist you on his back and take you leaping all over the field.'

'A frog! Ugh, just to hear you say it makes me feel queer!'

'Don't worry. In the land of the moon, the frogs never get up to mischief. Let me ask you a question. Didn't you meet the Byangama[67] bird on the way?'

'We certainly did!'

'How was that?'

'He swooped down from the top of the casuarina tree and stood straight up on his two feet. "Who dares carry off our Pupu-didi?" he demanded. No sooner had the rabbit heard him than he was off at top speed. He ran so fast that the Byangama bird couldn't catch him. What happened after that?'

'After what?'

'After the rabbit carried me off. Tell me what happened next.'

'How can I? *You're* the one who should tell *me*.'

'Now that's a fine thing to say! Wasn't I asleep? How should I know?'

'That's where the trouble lies, you see. I don't know where he's taken you. And if I don't know the address, which way am I to lead the rescue? All right, let me ask you something. As he bore you down the road, did you happen to hear any bells?'

'Yes, yes, they went ding-dong, ding-dong.'

'Then the road must have passed straight through the neighbourhood where the Bell-Ears live.'

'Bell-Ears! What are they like?'

'Their two ears are bells. And their two tails have hammers attached to their ends. With flicks of their tails, they ring a peal first on one ear, then on the other. Bell-Ears are of two species.

---

[67]*Byangama*: a mythical bird who, with his mate Byangami, often features in Bengali fairy tales.

One is the fierce kind, whose bells have brassy, warlike tones. The bells of the other toll with grave, booming notes.'

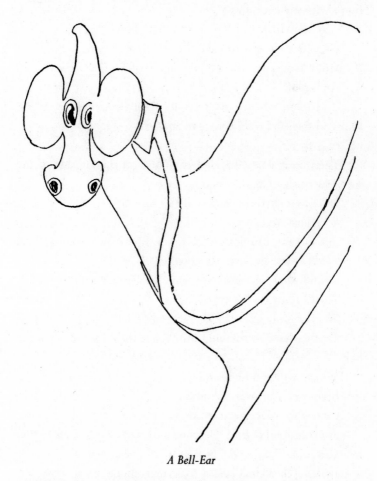

A Bell-Ear

'Do you ever hear their bells, Dadamashai?'

'I do indeed. Only last night, as I lay reading a book, I heard one striding through the darkness. When he had struck twelve,

I couldn't restrain myself. I dropped my book, started from my chair and ran to the bed. I buried my face in the pillow and lay there with my eyes shut tight.'

'Are the Bell-Ears friends with the rabbits?'

'Great friends. The sound of their bells guides the rabbit along the Milky Way, right through the home of the Seven Sages.'

'And then?'

'And then, when it strikes one, then two, then three and four and five, the road comes to an end.'

'And then?'

'Then he reaches the land of lights, on the far side of the meadow of sleep, and is seen no more.'

'Have I reached the land of lights too?'

'You must have.'

'In that case, I'm not on the rabbit's back any more?'

'You'd break his back if you were.'

'Oh, I forgot, I've become heavy once more. And then?'

'Then I must rescue you.'

'You certainly must. How will you do it?'

'That's what I'm thinking of. I think we'll have to seek the help of a prince.'

'Where will you find one?'

'Right here, in your Sukumar.'

At once your face grew grave. In rather a stiff tone, you said, 'You're very fond of him. He comes to recite his lessons to you every evening. That's why he's ahead of me in Maths.'

His being ahead may be due to certain other reasons. However, I refrained from dwelling on the topic. Instead, I said, 'Well, whether I'm fond of him or not, he's the only prince available.'

'How did you know?'

'After certain negotiations with me, he has confirmed himself in the post.'

You frowned heavily and said, 'All his negotiations seem to be with you.'

'What am I to do? He just won't accept that I'm a great deal older than him.'

'You call him a prince! I wouldn't even call him Jatayu.[68] Prince indeed!'

'Calm yourself a little: we've landed ourselves in great danger. We have no idea where you are. Let him carry out a rescue just this once, so that we can heave a sigh of relief. After that, I promise to turn him into a squirrel and set him to bridge-building.'

'Why should he agree to rescue me? He's busy studying for his exams.'

I have some hope that he'll agree. I'd gone to his home the Saturday before last. It was three o'clock in the afternoon. Having given his mother the slip, he was walking about on the terrace, in the blazing sun. I called up to him, 'What's the matter?'

He threw up his head and announced, 'I'm a prince!'

'Where's your sword?'

A broken stick from a half-burnt firework had been lying on their terrace ever since the night of Diwali. He had tied it to his waist with a ribbon, and now displayed it to me.

I said, 'A sword indeed! But you must have a horse as well!'

He answered, 'It's in the stables.'

So saying, he dragged out an ancient, shamelessly tattered umbrella of his uncle's from a corner of the terrace. He wedged

---

[68]*Jatayu*: a mythical bird. In the *Ramayana*, Jatayu carried to Rama the news of Sita's abduction by Ravana.

it between his knees, and with cries of 'Giddy up!' rode it round once at a gallop. I exclaimed, 'A noble beast!'

'Would you care to see its wings?'

'I certainly would.'

The umbrella opened with a swoosh. The feed-grains in its belly scattered all over the terrace.

I exclaimed, 'Astonishing! Marvellous! That I should have the fortune to see a real winged steed in this life surpasses all my hopes!'

'Now I'm flying, Dada. Keep your eyes shut, and you'll realize that I'm hovering by that cloud, right up there, in absolute darkness!'

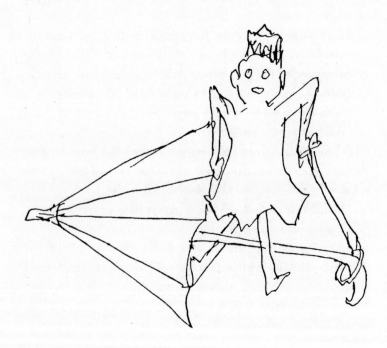

'I don't need to shut my eyes. It's quite clear to me: you're flying high, the wings of your steed are lost among the clouds.'

'Now Dadamashai, give my horse a name.'

'Chhatrapati,'[69] I suggested.

He answered for his horse, 'Yes, please, sir!'

Then he looked me in the face and said, 'You think I said "Yes, please, sir"? It wasn't me, it was the horse.'

'Do you think you have to tell me that? Am I deaf?'

The prince declared, 'Chhatrapati, I'm tired of sitting here quietly.'

From his own mouth came the reply, 'What is your command?'

'We must cross the field of Tepantar.'

'I'm ready.'

I could stay no longer—I had work to do. I was forced to bring the fun to an end. 'But, Prince, your tutor is waiting for you. I saw him—he's in a foul temper.'

The prince grew restless when he heard this. Thumping the umbrella, he demanded, 'Can't you fly off with me just now?'

I had to reply for the poor horse. 'He can't fly unless it's night. In the daytime he coyly disguises himself as an umbrella; he'll spread his wings as soon as you fall asleep. For the time being you'd better go in for your lesson, otherwise there'll be trouble.'

Sukumar went off for his lesson with the tutor. Before going, he warned me, 'I'm not done talking to you yet.'

---

[69]*Chhatrapati*: a title often used by kings, most famously by the Maratha hero Shivaji. It refers to the royal umbrella and therefore suits Sukumar's umbrella-horse.

I answered, 'Can a talk ever come to an end? Where's the fun, in that case?'

'My lesson gets over at five. Will you come then, Dadamashai?'

'After a session with the Third Class Reader, a first-class story is just what's needed to refresh the taste. I'll come,' I promised.

11

I SIGHTED THE TUTOR AT THE END OF THE LANE, EVIDENTLY WAITING FOR A tram. When I went back to Sukumar's house, it was half past five. The three-storey house opposite was shrouded in the glow of approaching twilight. I arrived to find Sukumar sitting silently in front of the room on the rooftop. Chhatrapati was resting in a corner of the terrace. The sound of my feet as I climbed the back stairs did not reach his ears. After a while I called, 'Prince!' He started, as if waking from a dream.

I asked, 'What are you thinking about, old fellow?'

He answered, 'The parrot and his mate.'[70]

'Now, where did you catch sight of them?'

'Away in the distance, where you see forests cloaking the hills. The branches are laden with flowers—yellow, red and blue, like clouds at sunset. From the depths of the branches come the voices of the parrot and his mate.'

'You can see them, can't you?'

'I can, but only partly. They're half-hidden by the leaves.'

'Well, what are they saying?'

This landed our prince in some difficulty. He said uncertainly, 'Please, Dadamashai, *you* tell me what they are saying.'

'Why, I can hear them quite clearly. They're arguing.'

---

[70]*The parrot and his mate*: *shuk* and *shari*, common figures in Bengali folk tales and songs.

'What about?'

'The parrot is saying, "I'm going to fly away now." His mate asks, "Where will you fly to?" The parrot answers, "To a place where they say there's nothing, nothing but flying. And you'll come with me."

'But his mate objects, "I love this forest; here, the passion-flower vines twine round the branches, clambering higher and higher; here one finds the fruits of the banyan. When the silk-cotton flowers bloom in this forest, I like to squabble over the honey with the crows. Here, at night, fireflies cast a shimmering veil over that clump of kamranga bushes; and in the monsoon, when the rain comes down in steady torrents, the coconut palms sway and their fronds brush against each other. What can one find in all your sky?" The parrot answers, "My sky holds both dawn and dusk, it holds the stars of midnight and the coming and going of the southerly breezes, and sheer emptiness—nothing, nothing at all."

Sukumar asked, 'How can there be nothing at all, Dadamashai?'

'That's exactly the question his mate is asking at this moment.'

'What does the parrot say to that?'

'The parrot replies that the sky's most priceless treasure is this nothing-at-all. "It's this nothing-at-all that calls to me at dawn. I pine for it as we build our nest in these woods. This nothing-at-all frolics in a riot of colours in the blue pastures of the sky. When the month of Magh is about to end, messages inviting the honeybees to come swarm along its tossing scarf and are carried swiftly on their way. The bees hear the call and stir joyfully."'

Sukumar leapt to his feet in enthusiasm. 'It's along the paths of nothingness that I must ride my horse,' he declared.

'Of course. Pupu-didi's abduction begins and ends in those magic fields.'

Sukumar clenched his fist. 'I'll bring her back through them, I swear I'll bring her back.'

'So you see, don't you, Pupu-didi?—The prince is quite ready, your rescue shan't be delayed. By now, his steed is testing its wings on the terrace.'

You flared up. 'There's no need.'

'What a thing to say! Until you're rescued from this grave danger, how can we be at peace?'

'I've been rescued already.'

'When?'

'Didn't you hear it? Just a little while ago, a Bell-Ear returned me to you.'

'When did all this happen?'

'Why, just as he rang nine peals on his bells.'

'What kind of Bell-Ear was he?'

'The fierce kind. Soon it'll be time to go to school. That's why his bells sounded so horrible.'

The story was thus broken off betimes. I should have hunted out some other prince. After all, this wasn't the kind of adding and taking-away one does in arithmetic: you couldn't bear the thought that the best boy in the class should have the audacity to cross the enchanted field of Tepantar. I'd already made up my mind to catch a hundred thousand of the crickets that haunt the undergrowth around our lotus pond. In huge swarms, they'd fly right through the west-facing windows of Uncle Moon's palace of sleep and tug at your bed sheet. Gently, they'd lower you onto it. Their droning would lull the watchman who guards the moon to sleep. I'd coax a band of torch-bearing fireflies to light your way. The crickets would carry you down a path through the bamboo grove; the dry leaves strewn over the ground would rustle and sigh. The fronds

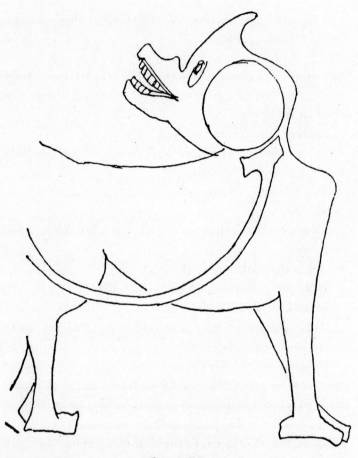

A fierce Bell-Ear

of the coconut palm would shudder and brush against each other. As you passed through the scented mustard-fields and reached Tirpurni's Ghat,[71] I would lure Mother Ganga's own makara[72] to

---

[71] *Tirpurni's Ghat*: a ghat (jetty or bathing place) mentioned in old rhymes and fairy tales.

[72] *makara*: a mythological aquatic animal, mount of the Goddess Ganga.

me with a bushel of the best paddy and put you on his back. The water would break into gurgling ripples as his tail cleft it, left and right. When the night reached its third hour, jackals would stand on the banks, and call, 'Whoo-oo goes by?' I'd scold them, 'Be quiet, no one goes by.' I'd have already made some discreet arrangements with the owl and the bat, and put them to use as well. At half past four, as dawn broke, the wishing star would droop low over the western horizon, but in the streak of light in the eastern sky, morning's pointing forefinger would be seen wearing a golden ring, whose scattered rays would signal the coming of day.

Pupu-didi smiled a little and said, 'About this story of my childishness that you've just told me—well, what pleasure did you get by twisting things so much? You seem very eager to show what a jealous creature I was! But as for my smuggling ripe fruit from our hog-plum tree to Sukumar-da, because he likes hog-plums—I faced the punishment for stealing them, while he tasted the rewards—you've left that out, haven't you? Perhaps Sukumar-da was quick at his sums, but I clearly remember the time when he couldn't think of the meaning of "cogitation", so I scribbled it on the back of my slate and showed it to him secretly. I suppose there's no room for all this in your story?'

I answered, 'What pleases me is not that you refused to accept Sukumar's princehood out of jealousy. You were jealous of him because of your love for me—that's what makes me happy when I remember it all.'

'Very well, you can keep your vanity to yourself. Let me ask you a question. What has become of that nameless man you made up, whom you used to call He?'

'He's grown older.'

'Good.'

'He's become a thinker. Worries buzz like hornets in his head, and have built a nest of cares. I can no longer match him in argument.'

'I see he's progressing on a line parallel to my own.'

'That may be so, but he's crossed the limits of fiction. Now and then, he clenches his fist and declares, "I must grow tougher!"'

'Let him. Let the story be built on a tougher skeleton this time. If we can't slurp it down, we'll at least be able to chew on it. Perhaps I'll like it better then.'

'I've kept him quiet all this time, for fear that your lack of wisdom teeth would make it hard for you to tackle him.'

'Dear me! Your fears make me laugh! You keep him away, and I'm the one not old enough!'

'Great heavens! Not even my worst enemy dares insult me so!'

'Then call him to your court, and let me judge his present mood.'

'So be it.'

12

I SAID TO JHAGRU, 'WHERE'S THAT MONKEY HE? WHEREVER YOU FIND him, call him here.'

He came, thumping his spiky staff of a stout rose-plant stem. His dhoti was tucked between his legs, his shawl wrapped around his waist. He wore knee-length socks of thick black wool and a sleeveless European waistcoat of green broadcloth over a red striped vest. On his head was a furry white Russian cap, bought at some second-hand shop, and his left thumb was bandaged with a strip of rag, clear witness to some recent rough-and-tumble. As he walked, the scrunch of his stout leather boots could be heard all the way from the corner of the lane. The eyes under his beetling brows were like a pair of bullets stopped in mid-flight.

'What's the matter?' he demanded. 'I was chewing on dried peas to strengthen my teeth, but your Jhagru wouldn't leave me alone. He said, "Babu's eyes are bloodshot, probably we'll have to call the doctor." As soon as I heard this, I rushed here with a jar of cow's piss from the cowshed. Take it in a banana-flower gourd and put it in your eyes drop by drop—they'll clear up in no time.'

I retorted, 'My eyes will remain bloodshot as long as you're around. All the important people from your neighbourhood have been laying siege at my door since early morning.'

'Why are you so upset?'

'If you're around, I don't need any other reason to feel upset.

I've had news that Kansari Munshi, the very sight of whose face
brings bad luck on a journey, is sitting on your roof, blowing on a
horn. You've lured a battalion of the hoarsest voices there with
the promise of ganja, and the assemblage is rehearsing its yells
with might and main. The gentlefolk are declaring their intention
of either quitting the locality themselves, or driving you out of it.'

He leapt up in great enthusiasm, bellowing, 'That proves it!'

'Proves what?'

'A combination of complete tunelessness and unequalled
vigour is absolute dynamite. Overpowering energy bursts forth
from the depths of discordance. Peace has fled and slumber taken
wing from the neighbourhood. Everywhere, people are vowing
to run away. The cacophony has unmistakably diabolic
associations. One day, even the worthy folk in heaven became
conscious of its impact. They were sitting with their eyes half-
closed, dreamily sipping nectar. The gandharva maestros[73] had
broken tunefully into taans[74] in the raga Paraj Vasant, tanpuras[75]
balanced against their shoulders. The apsaras[76] danced in expert
rhythm, amid a thunder of ankle-bells. Meanwhile, the demons
had sat for three long ages in the deathlike blue gloom of Hell's
chief mausoleum, fervently cultivating a tuneless furore while a
whale beat time with flicks of its tail. At last, one day, Saturn[77]

---

[73]*gandharva maestros*: heavenly singers, who sang before the gods.

[74]*taans*: long strings of notes sung or played as embellishments to classical
compositions.

[75]*tanpura*: a stringed instrument used to accompany songs or other instruments.

[76]*apsara*: celestial dancer.

[77]*Saturn*: the planet Saturn (Shani in Bengali) is believed to cast a baleful
influence upon the earth.

'That proves it!'

went into conjunction with this last degenerate age[78] to send out a signal for the screaming demons to descend upon the tuneful angels with all manner of bangs and thuds. Their tunelessness sizzled like a piece of eggplant cast into hot oil, prompting the gods to seek refuge in the inner chambers inhabited by Brahma's wife with cries of "grandfather, grandfather". I need tell you no more. I'm sure you're learned in the scriptures.'

'Your story has revealed my lamentable ignorance.'

'Dada, all your knowledge comes out of books, the real stuff never reaches your ears. Now I roam the cremation grounds, and pick up many little-known principles from their practitioners. From the blessed lips of my oddly toothed guru, I picked up some of the principles of tunelessness, after massaging his feet for several days with castor oil.'

'I realize it didn't take you long to imbibe the principles of tunelessness. I believe in the division of rights.'

'Dada, that's what I'm proud of. Being born male doesn't make you a man, you must possess the genius to become one. One day, from my Guru's divinely hideous lips—'

'A Guru's lips are said to be blessedly beautiful, and you call them divinely hideous!'

'My Guru's orders. He says that a beautiful face is weak, feminine. A hideous face is a man's pride. Its strength lies not in attraction but in repulsion. Don't you agree?'

'An unfortunate creature who's forced to agree can hardly do otherwise.'

'Your honeyed words have trapped you in a stupor, Dada—the harsh truth doesn't please your palate. You must break out

---

[78]*last degenerate age*: Kaliyug, the last and worst of the four mythical ages into which human history is divided in Indian mythology.

My Guru's divinely hideous lips

of this weakness that you sweetly call "good taste"—not being strong enough to stand the hideous.'

'It's much more difficult to break down a weakness than a strength. But you wanted to tell me what your Guru had said about the principles of tunelessness. Fire away.'

'My Guru began his explanation right from ancient times. He said, when man was about to be created, Lord Brahma the Four-Faced[79] produced a sweet tune from the lips on his two clean-shaven faces in front. Starting from the soft *re* and proceeding melodiously up the scale, slipping and sliding on a few smooth twists of the voice, he reached the soft *ni*.[80] This graceful wave of notes issued from the ruddy dawn clouds in the sky and set the sweet breeze swaying. In its gentle ripples, woman showed herself in the swaying rhythm of dance. Up in heaven, Lord Varuna's[81] wife began blowing on a conch-shell.'

'Why Lord Varuna's wife?'

'Why, she's the Goddess of Water. The race of woman is pure and fluid; not rigid, but lively and vivacious, even setting other things into motion. When the earth was being assembled, the ocean came first. The women floated about on its waters, mounted on cormorants.'

'Wonderful. But had cormorants been created by then?'

'Certainly. Why, it was in the voices of birds that the first sweet notes were being sung. It was these frail creatures' voices and wings that first proved how melody couldn't be separated

---

[79]*Lord Brahma the Four-Faced*: According to myth, Lord Brahma had five faces, one of which was burnt off by Shiva.

[80]*re, ni*: notes on the Indian musical scale, corresponding to *re* and *ti* on the Western.

[81]*Lord Varuna*: the Hindu god of water and the ocean.

from weakness. Let me tell you something. Promise you won't get angry.'

'I'll try not to.'

'At the beginning of the new age, when Grandfather God[82] created poets to bring mankind under the rule of weakness, he moulded them on the lines of the birds. That day there was a kind of literary gathering in his meeting hall and, as president, he exhorted all the poets who had gathered there to keep flying through space in their minds, to break into song for no reason at all, to turn everything unyielding into rippling liquid, to make soft what was sturdy. You're the King of Poets—you've obeyed his decree to this day.'

'I'll have to go on doing so, until I'm moulded differently.'

'The modern age is growing hard and dry; you won't get your soft waxen moulds any longer. The Goddess of Femininity no longer sits in a nest rocking on the water, swung back and forth by the swaying lotuses.[83] The world isn't sunk in the depths of languid delicacy.'

'Why didn't Creation stop once it reached that smooth rhythm?'

'Hardly had a few ages passed when the Earth-Goddess sent a pitiful appeal to Lord Brahma. She complained, "I can't bear the lolling grace of these ladies any longer." In rippling but afflicted tones, the women themselves declared that they were sick of it. From the higher regions came the question, "What are you sick of?" The maidens replied, "We don't know."—"What do you want?"—"We can't quite find that out either."'

---

[82]*Grandfather God*: refers to Lord Brahma.

[83]This image recalls the way the goddess Lakshmi is represented.

'Did the termagants among them keep quiet? Did they only speak sweet words from beginning to end?'

'There was no excuse for a quarrel, you see. There were no shafts of complaints to shoot off, so the bows remained sunk in the depths of the ocean, the twanging of their strings inaudible. No broomsticks to thwack anyone could sprout from the sea bed.'

'I suppose Lord Brahma was very ashamed at this sad news?'

'Without doubt. Why, all his four heads were bowed in shame. He sat in stunned silence upon the thousand-jointed wings of his swan[84] for a whole Brahmaic aeon.[85] But there was the celebrated priestess of ancient lore, the divine She-Cormorant, who, trying to match her colour with the pristine white of Lord Brahma's swan, had dived a thousand times into the water and rubbed at her feathers with her beak till they looked like cabbage-stalks thrown out into the garden for compost. Even she said, "Where there's too much mildness and decency, the chief delight of virtue is lacking, since you can't nag other people about their faults. You don't get any fun out of being good." She prayed, "O Lord, give us mean-mindedness immediately, in large and potent quantities." The Maker of Laws[86] sprang up in consternation, saying, "I've made a mistake—it must be corrected." That was it. What a voice! It was as if the Goddess Durga's lion had pounced upon Lord Shiva's bull,[87] and the furious roars of the lion were mingling

---

[84]*his swan*: All the gods and goddesses in the Hindu pantheon have animals for mounts; Brahma's is the swan.

[85]*Brahmaic aeon*: an immense tract of time. 4,320,000,000 human years constitute a single day for Brahma.

[86]*the Maker of Laws*: Brahma, referred to in the original as 'bidhi' or 'the maker of laws'.

[87]*Durga's lion, Shiva's bull*: In Hindu myth, the lion is Durga's mount and the bull is Shiva's.

with the tremendous bellows of the bull to crack the sapphire-studded foundations of heaven. The sage Narada hurried out, hoping for some fun. Thumping his threshing-stone on the back, he declared, "Threshing-stone, my son, listen carefully to this root of all future discord. It'll help us break up homes in due course." The celestial elephants that guard the ten quarters of the universe raised their trunks and added their trumpeting to Lord Brahma's furious four-throated roar. The sound was so powerful that the long hair of the Diganganas, the ten guardian goddesses of the earth, was swept loose and darkened the sky in billowing black clouds—it looked as if the sky was filled with the black sails of ships racing to Lord Yama's burning ghats.'

'Whatever you say, you can't deny that the Creator is male.'

'His masculinity could no longer be suppressed. The nostrils of his two bearded faces flared out like a pair of bellows. A storm cloud rushed scolding out of them to the four corners of the sky. That was when discord, with all its terrible force, was first released into the universe—roaring, thumping, grinding. The gandharvas shouldered their tanpuras and fled in hordes to Lord Indra's courtyard, where Sachidevi[88] retires after her bath to dry her hair in the fumes of parijat-scented[89] incense amidst the shade of a mandar[90] grove. The Earth-Goddess was sure she had made a horrible mistake: she trembled in fear as she recited the mantra to invoke beneficence. The erratic force of that storm of discord threw out male humans like fiery cannon balls.—You're very quiet, Dada. I hope my words are hitting you.'

'You may be sure they are. With loud thuds, too.'

---

[88]*Sachidevi*: Indra's wife.

[89]*parijat*: a celestial flower.

[90]*mandar*: a celestial plant.

'I hope you've understood that the crucial period of creation was ruled over by discord.'

'Do explain it to me.'

'The calm sovereignty of rippling water was overthrown— butted, elbowed, kicked, punched and pushed, as land reared its stony bald head. Wouldn't you agree that was the most important episode in the history of the earth?'

'I certainly would.'

'After all this time, the Creator's maleness had found expression in land; the seal of masculinity had been set upon the soil. What fearsome strength there was from the very start! Now stirring up flames, now freezing over with ice, sometimes splitting the ground open with the force of an earthquake and making it swallow down mountains as if they were doctors' pills—you'd admit there was nothing womanish in all that.'

'I certainly would.'

'The water broke into babbling waves, the wind whistled madly—but when the distressed land began to call, the sage Bharata's treatise on music[91] was squashed into a lump.—But you look as if you don't like this. What's bothering you?'

I said, 'All art is built upon an ancient foundation called tradition. Can you prove this art of tunelessness traditional?'

'Of course I can. The root of traditional tunefulness lies in a she-god's veena.[92] If you want to trace the origin of discord, walk straight past the ancient stronghold of women and pause at the he-god Shiva's threshold. At Kailash where he lives, the

---

[91]*sage Bharata's treatise on music*: the ancient sage, Bharata, composed the *Natyashastra*, which is regarded as the foundation of Indian classical music, drama and dance.

[92]*veena*: a stringed instrument.

veena is prohibited, and Urvashi[93] is never called in to dance. Shiva himself dances there—his furious dance of destruction, all out of time; his attendants Nandi and Bhringi blow horns, while the lord himself puffs out his cheeks and drums upon them with his fingers, or shakes his great rattle. Lumps of stone keep crashing down from Kailash's walls. I hope the ancient origin of grand disharmony is clear to you now.'

'It is.'

'Remember that the story of Daksha's Sacrifice in the Puranas,[94] where Shiva brings confusion to King Daksha's great ritual feast, centres upon the victory of discord over melody. All the gods and goddesses had once assembled at a banquet— rings in their ears, bracelets on their arms, jewels round their necks. The light danced off the forms of hermits and sages. Their voices rose in a hymn of faultless harmony. The whole universe thrilled to their song. All of a sudden, the tuneless brigade of everything ugly and hostile landed upon them, to the ruin of all the sweetness of this pious gathering. The victory of the hideous over the beautiful, the discordant over the melodious—the Puranas celebrate this principle with laughter and rejoicing, as you will notice if you leaf through the *Annadamangal*.[95] There you have it—the tradition of tunelessness, confirmed by the

---

[93]*Urvashi*: the most famous of the apsaras or celestial dancers. Rabindranath wrote a famous lyric poem addressed to Urvashi.

[94]*Daksha's Sacrifice in the Puranas*: The god Daksha arranged a great sacrificial rite to which Shiva and his wife Sati (Daksha's daughter) were not invited. Sati went to her father's home uninvited, and put an end to her own life when he began to abuse her husband. Hearing of his wife's death, Shiva had the feast destroyed and Daksha killed.

[95]Annadamangal: a poem by the eighteenth-century poet Bharatchandra Ray in praise of the goddess Annada, an aspect of Durga.

scriptures. Why, don't you see how eagerly everyone worships pot-bellied Ganesh? It's a stout protest against the beguiling gracefulness of art. Today, Ganesh's trunk has taken on the shape of a chimney and is trumpeting over the temples of manufacture in the West. Isn't it the loud tunelessness of that song that's bringing his devotees success? Think it over.'

'I will.'

'When you do, think over this as well—the invincible greatness of discord asserts itself on the hard soil. Lions, tigers, bulls—all those admirable creatures with whom heroes are compared—none of them ever practised the scales with an ustad. Any doubt of it?'

'None at all.'

'Even a humbler animal like the donkey, however weak, never professed intimacy with the veena-bearing goddess of musical circles[96]—a fact both friend and foe will readily admit.'

'That they will.'

'The horse has been tamed. Although its hooves are ideally suited to kick with, it suffers whipping without protest: it should have reared up on its hind legs in its stable and sung an alaap[97] in the Jhinjhitkhambaj raga. Its whinny might be a shower of foaming chandrabindus,[98] but in the discord of its

---

[96]*veena-bearing goddess of musical circles*: Saraswati, goddess of learning and music, who plays the veena and is therefore also called Veenapani (the veena-bearing one).

[97]*alaap*: a slow introductory passage played or sung at the start of a rendition of classical music.

[98]*chandrabindu*: in the Bengali alphabet, the mark placed over a letter to indicate its nasal intonation.

nasal tones, it doesn't forget to uphold the dignity of the land. And the elephant—we needn't even speak of him. All these land animals, disciples of Pashupati[99]—can you find a single songster among them? Your bulldog Freddy, who keeps the whole neighbourhood awake with his barking—if God, in jest or compassion, gave him the voice of a magpie-robin or shama bird, I'll bet he'd throw himself under the wheels of your motorcar, unable to stand the mockery of his sweet voice. Be honest: if a goat about to be sacrificed at Kalighat[100] sang a Ramkeli raga instead of bleating in fright, wouldn't you shoo it away disgustedly from the mother-goddess's sacred temple?'

'Of course I would.'

'Then you understand the import of the great vow we've taken. We're the devoted sons of firm land—we've received the sacrament of tunelessness. The world's already half dead; we intend to revive it with quackery. We need an awakening; we need strength! The movement's already started in the neighbourhood. The residents' vigour is growing more and more indomitable, issuing forth in biffs and thuds—my followers bear the proof on their backs. The guardians of the British Empire have bestirred themselves; the authorities are on the alert.'

'What does your Guru say to all this?'

'He's in a trance of rapture. His prophetic vision has shown him the coming of the worldwide renaissance of discord. All

---

[99]*Pashupati*: Shiva. The name Pashupati literally means 'lord of beasts'.

[100]*Kalighat*: a famous temple in Calcutta dedicated to the fierce goddess Kali, to whom blood-sacrifices are made.

civilized races are saying today that discord is reality, bursting
with maleness. Effeminate melody is what has weakened
civilization. What we need is not Christian meekness but force.
Discord is a rising power even in state legislation. Hasn't it struck
your eye, Dada?'

'Why should it need to strike my eye, brother? It's striking
my back, and hard too.'

'Meanwhile the twenty-five spooks of the old tale[101] have
mounted literature's back. Rejoice—Bengal's following in their
train.'

'Bengal's never hesitated to follow in anyone's train.'

'On the other hand, we've obeyed our Guru's order to
cultivate tunelessness by establishing a club, the Hoi! Hoi! Polloi.
A poet has joined the ranks—his appearance inspired us to hope
he was the New Age incarnate. His poems corrected our mistake:
he's one of your lot after all. We've told him a thousand times,
"Beat out the backbone of your verses with a club." "Reflect
constantly that all sense is but nonesense."[102] We explained to
him, "Respect for the meaning of words shows a slavish bent of
mind." No results. It's not the poor chap's fault; he breaks out in
a sweat, but just can't break out of that gentlemanly cut of his
poetry. We're keeping him on trial. I'll read you the first sample
of his skills that he showed us. But I can't sing it.'

'That's why I venture to let you into my room.'

---

[101]*old tale*: *Baital Pachisi*, an old Hindi story, translated into Bengali by
Ishwarchandra Vidyasagar.

[102]*Reflect constantly…*: from Shankaracharya's *Mohamudgar*. The original uses
the word *artha* in the sense of money, wealth. Rabindranath punningly applies
it in its other meaning, that is, sense, meaning.

'Then pay attention:

Man of music, leave your dwelling,
Run, instead, to distant reaches.
Flee from our impassioned yelling,
From our grunts and shrieks and screeches.
God and fiend have met to squabble
Over how the scales are sung:
The purest notes begin to wobble,
Bursting forth from every lung.
Sudden split in single raga,
Strings go *snap!* and rhythms swerve:
All day passes in this saga,
Beats thumped out with reckless verve.

'Our committee was up in arms: "This won't do. He's still
faithful to the conventions of his caste—weak pulse, compulsive
cleanliness. What we want is a reckless disregard for metre and
rhythm." We gave the poet some more time, and told him, "Gird up
your loins, and plunge into the fray one more time. Hammer the
message of power into the ears of Bengal's youth. Remember—
all over the world today, it is power that's pushing on relentlessly. Is
Bengal to stay asleep?" I realized the poet's insides were churning.
"Never, never!" he exclaimed. Chewing furiously on his pen, he
rushed to the table. With folded hands, he implored elephant-
headed Ganesh, "Send away your bride the banana tree.[103] O giver
of boons! Toss my brains with your trunk; let an earthquake attack
my mother tongue; let a turbid force erupt from my pen; let the
sons of Bengal wake to its harsh discordance!" Fifteen minutes later,

---

[103]Ganesh has a banana tree (*kalabou*) for a bride.

the poet burst out of his room and began to recite in a yell. His face was flushed, his hair in disarray—you should have seen him.

> Shout aloud the battle cry,
> Let your kicks and punches fly.
> Fierce Mar-hatta,[104] quickly come,
> Plunge into this bloody scrum.
> From this fight no stalwart spare,
> Pull them out from every lair.
> Rain down cuffs and blows and knocks,
> Bring your brickbats, stones and rocks,
> Smash your noses and your pates,
> Send your bones all to their fates.
> With your biffs and thuds and screams
> Rouse the sleepers from their dreams,
> Let them too, with angry yell,
> Fall on you and pound you well.
> Hush the singing of the flute:
> From the soil we must uproot
> With cruel wrench that gentle flower,
> Pride of Bengal's native bower,
> And in our gardens, give its place
> To jungle-creeper's sterner race.

'I threw up my hands in despair. "Stop, stop! Jayadeva's[105] spirits are still perched on your shoulders, conducting a circus of rhyme and rhythm, controlling your poetic ear. If you want to offer that poem to your dead ancestors at Gaya,[106] I'd advise you

---

[104]*Mar-hatta*: the warlike Maratha tribes who once inhabited present-day Maharashtra. The use of the archaic Mar-hatta allows a pun with the Bengali word 'mar' (beating).

[105]*Jayadeva*: a famous medieval Bengali poet, author of the *Gita Govinda*.

[106]*Gaya*: a place in Bihar believed to be specially propitious for the rites of the dead.

to grind it up with mortar and pestle, tear it, gnaw it, mortify it as much as you can, then spatter it with dots."

'The poet folded his hands and said, "I'm not equal to it—you take over."

'I said, "I see a faint glimmer of hope in your use of the word 'Mar-hatta'. But you've just yanked it out of the dictionary. The root of its meaning still lies buried—only the shoots of warlike sounds pierce through the soil. I'll throw it into disarray—note the shape that emerges.

Tally-ho Mar-hatta brave!
      Mutton-chop whiskers,
            Defiant of the smoothest shave.

Orchestra of grinding bones
      Squeak, squeak, screech.
      Rumble, rumble, rumble.
            Biff, bang, thud.

Cudgel
      Crash
            Out cold
            Compound fracture.

Bang.
Rumble tumble.
Deukinandan.
Jhanjhan Pandey.
Kundan the carter.
Banke Bihari.

Rattle-bang clip-clop.
Knock-knock flip-flop.
Bump bump.
Muffle scuffle.
Ho ho hoo hoo ha ha
P q r s t u v w x—
    Inferno Hades limbo.'

'Dada, I haven't forged your work—that you'll have to certify.'
'With pleasure.'
'You'll have to write the new epic of the New Age, Dada.'
'If I can. What's the subject?'
'The untuneful ogress Hirimba's Conquest of the World.'

I asked Pupu-didi how she liked it.
    'Rather confusing,' she answered.
    'In what sense?'
    'In the sense that I'm still wondering why I'm not disgusted by the victory of the demons over the gods. I feel strongly inclined to cast my vote in favour of those stubborn brutes.'
    'That's because you're a woman. Oppression still fascinates you. You're charmed by the strength of the person who beats you.'
    'Well, I can't say I like to be violently attacked—but when maleness assumes its most terrible form, fist upraised, it seems sublime.'
    'Let me tell you what I think. Manliness doesn't lie in a tyrannical flaunting of power—quite the contrary. To this day, it's been man that's created beauty and fought with the discordant. Evil pretends to be powerful only to the extent that man is cowardly. I find constant proof of this in the world today.'

13

PUPU-DIDI'S PRIDE WAS HURT. IN THE FALLING DUSK, SHE CAME AND SAT close to me, leaning on the arm of my chair. Looking the other way, she said, 'You keep making up childish stories about me. What pleasure do you get out of it?'

Nowadays, I lack the courage to laugh at her words. So I put on an affable expression and replied, 'At your age, you're all anxious to give proof of your mature wisdom. At my time of life, one likes to think that one's spirit is still young. So when I get the chance, I absorb myself in acts of made-up childishness. Perhaps they're unbecoming at times.'

'Well, if you're childish all the time, then it's not real childishness. The young always show signs of age.'

'Now that's a marvellous thing you've said, Didi. Even a baby's soft body has a frame of unyielding bone. How could I have forgotten this?'

'You seem to suggest that nothing happened in my childhood that was funny but needn't be made fun of.'

'Give me an example.'

'Think of our schoolmaster. He was peculiar, but peculiar through and through. That's why we liked him so much.'

'Do remind me of some of the things he used to say.'

'I remember his face clearly even today. In class, he seemed to be completely detached; he knew all the books by heart. His face turned upwards, he would reel off the lesson: it seemed as if the words were raining down from the heavens. He didn't seem bothered whether we attended class or listened attentively to the lesson: he was content to leave it to our discretion.'

'I suppose he didn't have much chance to get to know you by your faces.'

'He didn't even make the effort. One day, when I entered his room with a petition for a day's holiday, it put him in a nervous bustle. He hurriedly got up from his chair: he thought I was what you'd call a real, grown-up lady.'

'It was his habit to make these unimaginable errors.'

'It certainly was! I hope your beard didn't mislead him into thinking you the Nawab Khanzeh Khan's private secretary. But no more joking. He was your friend: tell me about him.'

'He had no enemies, but I was the only friend who really appreciated him. When people spread stories of his eccentricity, he would be amazed. One day, he came to me and said, "Everyone says that when I teach a class, I don't look at them as I teach."

'I said, "Your friends can't find fault with your learning, so they find fault with your acumen. They say that you don't forget what you teach. Instead, you forget that you're teaching."

'"If I didn't forget I was teaching, I wouldn't be able to teach. All I'd do would be what any plain schoolmaster does. I've completely digested the practice of teaching, my mind doesn't fidget over it any longer."

'"When an aquatic creature swims in the water, it doesn't attract attention; when a land animal does the same, it leaps to the eye. In the lake of learning, you're a fish of the deep waters."

'"If I look at the students, how am I to give my mind to the class?"

'"Where is that class of yours?"

'"Nowhere. That's why nothing interrupts me. If the students block my vision, I can't see the presiding spirit of the class."

'"'Ply your books, dear presiding spirit'—is that the maxim you teach?"

'"I don't teach! I simply let my own spirit circulate."

'"How do you manage that?"

'"The way the waters of the Ganga flow. On either side, there are deserts in some places, crops in others—cities, cremation grounds. If Mother Ganga had had to take a decision at every step, she would never have saved the children of Sagar.[107] What happens to one is what's destined to happen: vying with God to force more happenings only holds up the flow. My teaching flows through space like the clouds. The rain falls from it on many fields, but the harvest each one bears depends on the field. The headmaster is vexed because I don't waste time trying to push through the impossible. To count this headmaster as eminently real would be eminently foolish."'

Pupu-didi said, 'Lots of his pupils felt uneasy about him. He told them one day, "This master that you have here, I've erased him, so as to give your own minds the space to grow in." Another day he remarked, "When it comes to teaching, I'm a classicist and Sidhu-babu a romantic." Needless to say, we couldn't make head or tail of his words.'

---

[107]*children of Sagar*: The mythical King Sagar had 60,000 sons, who insulted a sage and were burnt to death by the fire of his anger. However, Sagar's descendant Bhagirath was able to please Shiva and bring Ganga to the earth, whose waters, flowing over the ashes of the men, set them free.

'It means your teacher hoisted the entire class higher, while Sidhu carried one pupil at a time on his shoulders across potholes. Do you understand now?'

'No, and I don't need to either. Go on about him, it's fun to hear.'

'It amuses me too, because it takes a while to understand the man. One day he declared, quoting a Chinese philosopher, "The state that exists without rule is the best of all states."'

Pupe declared with pride, 'There's no doubt that our class was the best in the school.'

I replied, 'That was because your master refused to notice the signs of your mean intelligence, despite clear proof of dim-wittedness.'

Pupu-didi tossed her head. 'Am I to call this an insult or a joke?'

I answered, 'It's a joke of the milder sort, as if I were to tweak your hair in passing. It doesn't declare *casus belli*—none of your "It's battle today between you and me".'

Pupe continued, 'Mastermashai's methods were of a funny kind. "You must keep your own records," he used to say. "It's not my business to check on you." We used to keep a daily log of our work; we knew the system of marking.'

'What was the result?'

'We gave ourselves lower marks, as a matter of fact.'

'Didn't you ever cheat him?'

'If someone else had been marking us, we might have been tempted to cheat. It would have been foolish to cheat oneself, especially since he never checked on us.'

'And then?'

'And then, after every three months we'd do our own calculations and find out for ourselves if we had gone up or down.'

'Was yours an especially high high-school of the Age of Truth?[108] Wasn't there anyone who indulged in a little deceit?'

'Mastermashai remained unperturbed. He would say, "Some people in this world are bound to shirk and cheat, but those responsible for themselves are less likely to do so." Our punishments were of the same kind, never externally inflicted. One day, during roll call, I lied to save my best friend's record of attendance. He said to me, "You've been dishonest: you must perform a penance." He didn't even want to know, later, if I'd performed it.'

'And did you?'

'I certainly did.'

'Meaning, you gave away your powder box to your friend?'

'I never use powder.'

'You mean to say that complexion of yours is entirely your own?'

'Whatever else, at least I haven't borrowed it from you, as you'll realize if you try to compare the two.'

'For shame! If you see a difference in our complexions, you're finding fault with our entire clan. We're of the same blood; our complexions can't ever be dissimilar. Had there been a poet at hand, he would have declared that your colour had sprung from Lord Brahma's smile.'

'And yours from his sneer.'

'This is what's called anyanyastuti, mutual admiration. Grandfathers have two kinds of smiles—one dental, the other cerebral. It's the cerebral kind that fell to me—what one calls wit in English.'

'Dadamashai, you never stop singing your own praises.'

---

[108]*Age of Truth*: Satyayug, the first and best of the four mythical ages.

'That's my chief virtue. I belong to the band of exceptional men who know themselves.'

'Your tongue's wagging again. But no more; please stop now. We were talking about the schoolmaster, now we've begun to talk about you.'

'What's wrong with that? The subject is congenial, what in English you might call *interesting*.'

'That subject is always there in front of me. I don't have to remember it. Rather, it's difficult to overlook.'

'All right, let me tell you about a special side of this teacher of ours. It's worth writing down. Once the master had invited some people home for the evening. To see if he remembered having done so, I went to his house, quite early in the morning. Let me tell you of the conversation he was having with his servant Kanai.

'Kanai said, "Lobsters are very expensive now, because of Jagaddhatri Puja.[109] So I've bought egg-laden crabs instead."

'The schoolmaster asked, slightly worried, "What'll you do with the crabs?"

'Kanai replied, "I'll put them in a curry with gourd, they'll taste delicious."

'I asked, "Master, do you have a special craving for lobsters?"

'The master answered, "I certainly do."

'"Well, in that case, you'll have to restrain it!"

'"Why restrain it? The desire's ready at hand, all I need do is shunt it in the direction of the crabs."

'"I see you have to do a good deal of shunting."

'The schoolmaster said, "I've eaten crab curry many times. I

---

[109]*Jagaddhatri Puja*: the festival of the goddess Jagaddhatri, one of the forms assumed by Durga.

never put my whole mind to it. But now that I've seen Kanai's mouth water, my mind will turn towards the crab at dinnertime, guided by his drooling tongue: it'll add to the relish. It's as if he'd underlined the curry in red pencil; it'll help me to memorize it."

'The master asked, "What have you got tied up in that bundle?"

'"Drumsticks," said Kanai.

'The master looked at me and said with pride, "There's the fun of it. When he went to the market, I was thinking of gourd stems. Now that he's back, I've got drumsticks instead. That's the advantage of never giving orders."

'"What if, instead of drumsticks, he'd brought back snake-gourds?" I asked.

'The master answered, "In that case, I'd have felt a moment's qualm. You see, the name has an influence on the matter. The name 'snake-gourd' isn't appetizing. But if Kanai had chosen it specially, it would have given me a chance to overcome my instincts. For the first time in my life, I'd have had the chance to think, 'Why not try it and see?' Perhaps I'd have discovered that it wasn't bad after all. My blind prejudice against the vegetable would have been removed, and the limits of my enjoyment extended. That's how poets, in their works, try to extend our tastes to share their own. Their work is to underline the process of creation."

'"Does Kanai have any hand in trying to expand the limits of your taste?"

'"He certainly does. If it hadn't been for him, I wouldn't ever have paid any attention to piring-shaak.[110] The very word would

---

[110]*piring-shaak*: a kind of edible leaf.

have knocked me over. In this world, freedom from prejudice means widening one's vision."

'"And your Kanai is engaged in that worthy task."

'"You've got to admit that, brother. By adding his desires to mine, my own lose their narrowness. If I'd been living on my own, this could never have happened."

'"I understand, but the limits of Kanai's desires—"

'"I've widened them. He comes from East Bengal, and couldn't stand the mention of kalai dal.[111] Nowadays he's quite happy to eat it cooked with asafoetida."

'Suddenly, at this point, Kanai entered again. He said, "I forgot to tell you that I haven't brought any curd today. The kaviraj has forbidden curd at night."

'Since he didn't want to repeat himself by saying that the price of curd too had risen, he had had to hatch the tale involving the kaviraj. As consolation, he promised, "I'll make you some weak tea with a little juice of ginger in it; it'll be good for you in the cold night."

' "What do you say, Master?" I asked. "Thinking of offering everyone some tea with ginger?"

' "How can I answer for everyone? Those who'll drink it will drink it. It might do them good. As for those who won't, it won't do them any harm."

'I asked, "According to the teachings of the Chinese philosophers, your household admits no master, does it?"

'"No."

'"Then how can you accept a servant?"

'"If there's no master, there obviously can't be a servant."

---

[111] *kalai dal*: a kind of lentil.

'"I suppose you've mixed up master and servant to create a compound substance?"

'The schoolmaster smiled. "Oxygen and hydrogen lay aside their incendiary natures and mingle to form water."

'I retorted, "Had you married, brother, all your Chinese philosophy would have fled the town. A wife isn't so ethereal an entity as to exist, yet not to exist. Even though her face might be demurely veiled, her presence would be a very tangible truth. Under her rule, the kingdom would reel at a frown from her eye: you'd be subject to constant buffeting, front and back."

'The schoolmaster replied, "In that case, the husband would escape to Dera Ghazi Khan[112] on a one-way ticket, while his spouse's wifeliness disappeared down the tracks of the East Bengal Railway as she returned to her father's home."

'The schoolmaster sometimes says funny things, but never laughs.'

'If you had to make up a story about our teacher, how would you go about it?' asked Pupu-didi.

'I'd have to set aside a million years!'

'That means you'd make up some fantastic tale. But you wouldn't have to worry about your present-day critics.'

'No man of letters fears such witnesses. The truth is, my story will need a change of era to come alive. Let me explain why. The basic materials in the creation of the world were stone, iron and other such heavy stuff. The business of moulding these, hammering them into shape, went on for ages. Their hardness remained bare and exposed for many ages. At last, soft earth

---

[112]*Dera Ghazi Khan*: a town and district now in Pakistan, in the very opposite direction to that served by the East Bengal Railway.

covered the surface in a carpet of green; as if to protect the dignity of the creator. Then the animals made their appearance; they roamed the earth bearing vast burdens of bones and flesh, wearing heavy suits of armour, and dragging indecently heavy tails. They were spectacular beasts. But these flesh-burdened creatures didn't meet the Creator's approval. He began his relentless experiments once again, and kept at it age after age. At last came man, who possessed a mind. The unnecessary tail disappeared, bones and flesh remained only in modest quantities, and the tough hide was softened into skin. No longer were there horns, or hooves, or the fierce power of talons. The four legs were reduced to two. It was understood that the Almighty was plying his tools to refine the Age of Creation more and more. Man is entangled in both the crude and the fine. The struggle between mind and flesh goes on. In fact, the Almighty is shaking his head again: 'No, this hasn't turned out right.' There are signs that this age too will not last long. It will destroy itself through a supreme scientific expedient. A few hundreds of thousands of years will go by. Gradually, the flesh will fall away and the mind will emerge supreme. It is in this age of the perfect mind that your master sits, in a class of bodiless pupils. Just think how his method of teaching was to merge himself in his pupils, spreading one mind over the other as though there were no external hindrances.'

'Not even that of the material senses?'

'If that weren't there, the intelligence would find itself with nothing to do. There's always a difference between good and bad, stupid and clever. Human character is of many types. There are varieties of thought and singularities of desire. He who can enter these disparate worlds makes a good schoolmaster. Education is now an inner process.'

'Dadamashai, I can't remember just where this school is.'

'The world has three homes—one beneath the ocean, one on land, and one in the sky, with subtle winds and subtler light. This last one is empty at present: it's reserved for the next era.'

'In that case, your class is being wafted along on that wind, that light. But what do the students look like?'

'It's hard to explain. They certainly have forms, but the forms are unconfined.'

'Then I suppose they're made of various-coloured lights.'

'That's possible. Didn't the science master explain to you the other day how, in this very universe, fine particles of light are pretending to take on bodily form, like chameleons? But at that time, light will find expression in its own original, ethereal form. All of you will sit radiating light in class. That day, sellers of Otin Snow[113] will go bankrupt.'

'Why should they go bankrupt? They'll turn into light.'

'To go bankrupt means to turn into light.'

'What colour will I be, Dadamashai, when I turn into light?'

'Golden.'

'And you?'

'I'll be pure radium.'

'There won't be any fighting among the lights that day, will there, Dadamashai? Is there likely to be any squabbling over electrons?'

'You've got me worried. We'll probably need a League of Lights. I can already hear rumours of quarrelling over electrons.'

'All the better, Dadamashai. You'll be able to render the

---

[113]*Otin Snow*: a face cream popular at the time.

martial spirit eloquently in your poem. Oh dear, will there be language, though?'

'The language of words will simply transform into the language of feeling. You won't have to memorize any grammar.'

'What about songs?'

'Music must conform to colour. It won't be very easy. The taans will dart to all corners of the sky. The Tansens[114] of the age will light up the horizon with a new aurora borealis.'

'And what'll happen to all your free verse?'

'Electrons of iron and of gold will mingle in them.'

'The grandmothers of that age will disapprove.'

'I have a feeling that all the granddaughters of the time will be enthralled.'

'In that case, I'll take care to be born your granddaughter in that Age of Light as well. For the present, you'll have to bear with this bearer of flesh and form. Now I'm off to the cinema.'

'What's the film?'

'*Sita's Exile.*'

---

[114] *Tansen*: a singer of legendary fame, one of the 'nine jewels' of the Mughal Emperor Akbar's court.

14

NEXT MORNING, PUPE-DIDI BROUGHT ME BREAKFAST AS I HAD ORDERED: chickpeas and molasses in a stone bowl. I'd set about reviving ancient Bengali cuisine in this modern age. Didimani asked, 'What about tea?'

I answered, 'No, date palm juice.'

Didi asked, 'Why are you looking so sombre today? Did you have a bad dream?'

I replied, 'The shadows of dreams constantly pass over my mind—then the dreams dissolve and the shadows disappear. Today, I keep remembering a story of your childishness: I'd love to tell you.'

'Do.'

'That day, I'd stopped writing and was sitting on the veranda. You were there, so was Sukumar. Darkness fell, the lamps on the streets were lit, and I sat there making up stories of the Age of Truth for you.'

'Making up stories! That means you were turning it into the Age of Falsehood!'

'Don't call them false. A ray of light that has crossed the limits of violet can't be seen; but you can't say it doesn't exist— it's just as much light. It's in that ultraviolet glow of history that man has created his Age of Truth. I wouldn't call it prehistoric— rather, it is ultra-historic.'

'You needn't explain any more. Go on with what you were saying.'

'I was telling you that in the Age of Truth people didn't learn things out of books, or from reports. Their knowledge just grew of itself, out of being.'

'I don't understand what you mean.'

'Listen to this carefully. You probably believe that you know me?'

'I do indeed.'

'You do know me, but that knowing lacks ninety-nine and a half per cent of real knowing. But if you could, within yourself, become me whenever you wished, your knowing would be complete and true.'

'In that case, you'd like to say that we don't know anything at all?'

'We certainly don't. We've all assumed that we know things, and all our work is founded upon this collective assumption.'

'Well, the work seems to be going pretty well.'

'It's going along, but this going-along doesn't belong to the Age of Truth. That's what I was telling you: in the Age of Truth, people didn't know by seeing or touching, but by absolutely being.'

The feminine mind always clings to solid proof; I'd thought my idea would strike Pupu as utterly fantastic and that she wouldn't like it, but it appeared to rouse her curiosity. She said, 'That's rather fun.'

Then she got quite excited, and asked, 'Dadamashai, nowadays science claims to do a lot of things. We listen to the songs of dead people, see the faces of people far away—I even hear of lead being turned into gold. Perhaps one day it'll work such a trick with electricity that one person will be able to mingle with another.'

'It's not impossible. But what will you do then? You won't be able to hide anything from me!'

'Good heavens! Everyone's got lots to hide.'

'It's because we hide them that there are things to hide. If no one had anything hidden away, everyone would carry on knowing everything about everyone else, like a card game where you can see everyone's hands.'

'But there are lots of things to be ashamed of.'

'If all shameful things were revealed, the sense of shame would lose its edge.'

'All right, but what were you going to say about me?'

'The other day, I asked you what you'd have liked to see yourself as, if you'd been born in the Age of Truth. You blurted out—"An Afghan cat!"'

Pupu grew very cross and declared, 'Never! You're making it up!'

'My Age of Truth may be my creation, but your words are yours alone. Not even a talkative old fellow like me could make them up all of a sudden.'

'I take it you thought me very stupid because of my wish.'

'I only thought you very much wanted an Afghan cat but had no chance of acquiring one, as your father can't stand cats. In my view, in the Age of Truth, you wouldn't have to buy a cat, or possess one; you could just turn yourself into a cat at will.'

'First a human, then a cat—what good would that do? Even buying a cat would be better than that, or doing without one if you couldn't buy it.'

'There, you see, your mind can't quite grasp the wonder of the Age of Truth. The Pupe of the Age of Truth would extend the limits of her being to include those of a cat. You wouldn't be robbed of your limits. You'd be yourself—and the cat as well.'

'There's no meaning to these speeches of yours.'

'In the language of the Age of Truth, they have plenty of meaning. The other day, your teacher Pramatha-babu told you that the molecules that make up light are a shower of tiny particles, like rain; and at the same time, a current of flowing waves, like a river. Our ordinary intelligence tells us, "either this, or that", but the scientific mind accepts both at the same time. In the same way, at the same time, you're both Pupu and the cat—so says the Age of Truth.'

'Dadamashai, the older you grow, the more incomprehensible your words become—just like your poems.'

'A pointer to the time when I'll become completely silent.'

'Didn't our conversation that day go any further than the Afghan cat?'

'It did. Sukumar was sitting in the corner. He said dreamily, "I'd like to try being a sal tree."

'You were always happy to have a chance to laugh at Sukumar. Hearing he wanted to be a sal tree, you laughed yourself sick. He started in shame. So I took the poor chap's side, and said, "Imagine—the southerly wind begins to blow—the branches of the tree are covered with flowers, an invisible charm flows through its veins, with a constant play of beauty and sweet scent. How dearly we wish to feel this passion from within! If you can't be a tree, how can you feel the boundless thrill of a tree in springtime?"

'Hearing my words, Sukumar grew excited. He declared, "You can see a sal tree from my bedroom window. When I lie in bed, I see its crown, and it seems as if it's dreaming."

Sukumar

'On being told that a sal tree was dreaming, you were probably about to exclaim, "What a silly thing to say!" To stop you, I went on, "A sal tree's whole life is a dream. It passes in a dream from seed to seedling, from seedling to tree. Even its leaves are the words it has spoken in its dream."

'I said to Sukumar, "The other day, on that cloudy, rainy morning, I saw you standing on the northern veranda, clutching the railing. What were you thinking of?"

'Sukumar answered, "Why, I don't know what I was thinking of."

'I said, "Those unknown thoughts had filled your mind, just as the clouds filled the sky. The trees stand still in just the same way, as if lost in some unknown thought or emotion. Those thoughts darken among the monsoon clouds and gleam in the sunshine of a winter morning. The new leaves start to babble in the language of those thoughts; the flower buds and blossoms begin to sing."

'I still remember how Sukumar's eyes grew wide with pleasure. "If I could be a tree," he said, "the murmur of the leaves would quiver through my body and drift up into the clouds."

'You noticed that Sukumar had taken centre stage. Pushing him into the wings, you stepped into the limelight, and asked, "Dadamashai, if the Age of Truth arrives, what would you like to be?"

'You thought I'd want to be a mastodon or a megatherium, since I had discussed the early history of the animal kingdom with you only the other day. The earth was very young and tender then, and the continents hadn't hardened into solid masses. The plants and creepers had been painted with only the first strokes of the Creator's brush. You had heard me say that in those ancient forests, ruled over by uncertain, ever-changing seasons, creatures evolved in a manner hard for us to imagine today. You had realized from my words how desperately man longs to know more of that epic age when life made its first foray into the world. So if I had suddenly yelled, "I'd like to be one of those prehistoric hairy four-tusked elephants," you'd have been happy. It would have been like your wish to be an Afghan cat—I'd have belonged to your group. In the normal way, I might not have disappointed you. But Sukumar's words had drawn my mind in another direction.'

'I know, I know,' said Pupe. 'Sukumar-da's thoughts were always much closer to yours than mine.'

'The only reason for that,' I said, 'is that he was a boy, just as I had been. His imagination had been shaped in the same mould as my own childish fancy. When you sat down with your toy pots and pans to build the happy household of your dreams, you were well content. But I could only observe your dream from a distance. When you danced your play-child on your knee, it was beyond me to grasp the immensity of your love.'

'Never mind all that now,' said Pupu. 'Tell me what you wanted to be that day.'

'I had wanted to be a bit of the landscape, stretched over a wide expanse. It's the hour of dawn, and now that the month of Magh is drawing to a close the wind is restless. In the tossing wind, the old ashvatthva tree seems as lively as a child; the waters of the stream have broken into a soft babble and the trees stand in shadowy groups on its rolling banks. Behind all this stretches the open sky, and it has a faraway look—as if a bell is ringing on the far bank of that empty distance, the notes half-blown away by the wind, its message mingling with the sunshine: the hour passes.

'The look on your face showed clearly that you thought wanting to be a complete landscape—stream, woods and sky— a great deal more outlandish than wanting to be a single tree.

'Sukumar spoke. "It's fun to think of you spreading over trees and streams and becoming part of them. Do you think there ever will be an Age of Truth?"

'"Till it arrives, we have paintings and poems. They are wonderful paths down which you can forget yourself and become other things."

'"Did you ever draw a picture of what you've just told us about?" asked Sukumar.

'"I did."

'"I'm going to draw one too."

'His audacity made you angry. "I doubt if *you'll* ever be able to draw anything!"

'"Of course he will," said I. "When you've finished the painting, old chap, I'll take yours and you shall have mine."

'That's as far as our conversation went that day.

'Let me tell you the last thing we discussed that day. You had gone off to feed your pigeons. Sukumar was still sitting there, thinking deeply. I said to him, "Shall I tell you what you're thinking of?"

'"Let's see you do it," said he.

'"You're trying to think of all the other things it might be fun to become—perhaps the rain-soaked monsoon sky, darkening as the first clouds gather, or maybe the little sailing boat racing homeward as the Pujas approach. While we're on the subject, let me tell you of a story from my own life. You know how I used to love Dhiru. One day, like a bolt from the blue, I received a telegram saying he was very ill with typhoid. I rushed to his house in Munshigunj that very evening. A week went by. The day was oppressively hot, with the sun blazing overhead. A dog howled mournfully in the distance, making me feel melancholy. Evening fell, and the sun sank slowly. The fig tree in the west cast its shadow on the veranda. The neighbourhood milk-woman came and asked, 'How is Khoka-babu today?' I answered, 'His headache is better, and so is the pain in his limbs.' Some of the people taking care of him got a chance to rest. Two doctors came and examined him, then stood outside the room talking in whispers; I realized there was no hope for him. I sat there quietly, feeling it useless to listen. The evening shadows darkened. The evening star shone above the immense neem tree before me. I could no longer hear the rumble of the jute-laden bullock carts on the distant road. There seemed to be a droning in the sky. I don't quite know why I kept saying to myself, 'From the western sky comes peace, made manifest in night—cool, dark, still. Darkness comes at the end of each day, but today it seems to have a special form and touch.' I closed my eyes, and let the slowly approaching darkness wash over my mind and body, saying inside me, 'O peace, O night, you are my Didi, my sister of ages without end. As you stand waiting at sunset's door, draw my little brother Dhiru to your breast; relieve him of his suffering.' A wail rose from the attendants standing beside the sickbed; the doctor's carriage wound its way home down the silent street. That day, I felt night spread across my mind—I let it envelop me, just as the world submits to the reign of its all-veiling, meditative calm."

'I don't know what Sukumar thought of all this. He declared eagerly, "But your Didi will never steal me away in the darkness. When the Puja holidays come, and no one has to go to school even at ten in the morning—when the boys play cricket in the chariot square—on one of those days, I'll just melt away into the sunshine of a holiday morning, almost as if in play."

'I listened in silence. I didn't utter a word.'

Pupe-didi said, 'Ever since yesterday, you've been talking of no one but Sukumar-da—usually poking a little fun at me in the process. Do you think he and I are still rivals for your affection, as we were when we were children?'

'Perhaps you are, a little bit. That's why I keep speaking of him—to wipe away the last traces of your jealousy. There's also another reason.'

'Well, why don't you tell me what it is?'

'A few days ago, Sukumar's father Doctor Nitai came to say goodbye.'

'Goodbye? Why goodbye?'

'I had thought of telling you, but never got around to it. I will today. Nitai wanted Sukumar to read law, but Sukumar wanted to learn painting under Nandalal-babu.[115] Nitai said, "Painting might keep your fingers busy, but it won't feed your stomach."

'"My hunger for painting is far greater than the hunger of my stomach," said Sukumar.

'Nitai said with some sternness, "You've never had to prove that yet—you've never had to earn your bread."

'His father's words fell harshly on his ears, but all the same, Sukumar smiled and said, "You're right—I should prove my words."

'The father thought his son would now settle down to the law at last. Sukumar's maternal grandfather at Barishal[116] is a rather eccentric old man, and Sukumar resembles him in both looks and character. The two were the best of friends. They discussed

---

[115]*Nandalal-babu*: Nandalal Bose, a famous artist, who at this time was the head of Kala Bhavan, the art department of Tagore's university, Visva-Bharati.
[116]*Barishal*: a district of Bengal now in Bangladesh.

the matter between them. Sukumar received some money, and slipped away abroad before anyone knew it. He left a letter for his father: "You don't want me to study painting. Very well, I shan't. You want me to learn a trade, and that's what I've set out to do. When my training is complete, I'll come to you for your blessings. I hope to receive them."

'But he had told no one what trade he intended to learn. A diary was found in his desk. From its contents, his family realized that he'd gone to train as a pilot. I brought away a copy of the last pages of his diary. He had written:

'"I remember embarking upon a journey from one end of our terrace to another, on my faithful winged horse Chhatrapati, to rescue Pupu-didi from the land of the moon. Now I'm setting off to tame a mechanical winged horse. In Europe, they're preparing to send an expedition to the moon. If I get a chance, I'll put my name down for it. For the moment, I'm content to hone my skills by flying round the earth. One day, Pupu-didi laughed at the picture I'd painted in imitation of her grandfather's. From that day on, for ten whole years, I've practised painting. I've never shown anyone my pictures. I'm now leaving behind two I drew recently for her grandfather. One is about the unity of earth, water and sky; the other a portrait of my grandfather at Barishal. If Pupe's Dadamashai can make her take back that day's laugh by showing her the two pictures, well and good. If not, he should tear them up and throw them away. This time, it's not impossible that my horse's wings should break halfway on the road to the moon. If they do, I'll reach the Land of Truth in the blink of an eyelid—my journey round the sun will end in my melting into the earth. If I survive and become adept at paddling my boat across the sky, I hope one day to take Pupu-didi with me on a journey into space. I seem to remember that in the Age of Truth, what you wanted was exactly what happened. I'll try to train my mind to see desire as result. Since childhood, I've had the habit of gazing idly at the sky, filled as it is with the million wishes of the earth-bound. I wonder what use these fleeting wishes are in creating new worlds. Let the unspoken wishes that float upon my sighs drift in that sky, the sky I am myself about to fly in today."'

Pupu-didi asked in distress, 'What news of Sukumar-da now?'

I answered, 'It's because there isn't any that his father's going to England to look for him.'

Pupu-didi's face fell. Quietly, she went to her room and closed the door.

I know Pupu-didi has hidden away those childish drawings of Sukumar's in her desk.

I wiped my spectacles and went off to Sukumar's house. The broken umbrella was no longer on the terrace, neither was the half-burnt stick.